MINDS

Also by David Black

MURDER AT THE MET
THE KING OF FIFTH AVENUE
LIKE FATHER
EKSTASY

MINDS

DAVID BLACK

TIMBRE BOOKS • ARBOR HOUSE
NEW YORK

 Published in the United States of America by Arbor House Publishing Company and in Canada by Fitzhenry & Whiteside, Ltd.

Manufactured in the United States of America

10 9 8 7 6 5 4 3 2 1

Library of Congress Cataloging in Publication Data
Black, David, 1945-
  Minds.

  I. Title.
PS3552.L32M48 1985 813'.54 84-24272
ISBN 0-87795-703-7

Minds is a work of fiction. Any similarity between characters and places in this book and those in real life is coincidental.

For Deborah and Susannah

ABRAHAM: 1909

Chapter 1

By the time Abraham Gottenberg reached Galilee, Nebraska, on September 16, 1909, he had already forgotten what Sigmund Freud looked like. When he tried to reassemble the face in his memory, he saw a bearded mask that fit imperfectly and hid the features. Only the eyes, sunk behind the holes in the mask, and the large, fleshy ears, which reminded Abraham of his father's, seemed real.

But he had no trouble recalling Freud's lectures and the oddly informal tone in which they had been given. A bedtime-story voice, Abraham had thought, and he had listened with the exhilaration of a child who wants to believe the wonders he is being told, no matter how improbable they seem. Freud had given five talks at Clark University in Worcester, Massachusetts. When Abraham left Clark at the end of the week, he was so excited by what he'd heard that he forgot to wire home to have one of his sons meet him at the railroad station.

Abraham arrived early in the morning. He slipped his

watch from his waistcoat pocket. Two o'clock. Unbalanced by his heavy gladstone bag, he lurched down the aisle of the sleeping car. The bunks with their closed curtains looked like marionette theaters. The murmurs, sighs, and grunts of the hidden sleepers betrayed the private dramas being performed in dreams, rehearsals for the shows that would begin in the morning when the sleepers woke. The air in the car was stale with old cigar smoke and sweat. Abraham's woolen long johns itched. When the train stopped, he was glad to step into the chilly wind.

The train chuffed off, embers starring the night sky. Abraham left his bag at the station house. Carrying it would slow him down. He would send for it tomorrow. He crossed the wooden platform, leaped off the end, and hurried along the path beside the tracks, which, although the train was by now far down the line, still ticked with the sound of turning wheels. Where the path became boggy, Abraham scrambled up a slope, on all fours at its steepest part, his beard brushing the top of the tall grass. He heaved himself over a fence and trotted through a backyard. Reaching the road that led out of town to his house, he started to run.

Abraham was fifty years old. Never before in his adult life had he taken a shortcut.

When Jacob Gottenberg, Abraham's oldest son and like his father a doctor, heard the front door slam, he thought it was a shot, although no one in the house owned a gun. Jumping from bed, he opened his door and saw his father, his beard prickly with snagged burrs, looming out of the hall shadows toward him.

"Get dressed," Abraham said in German, his native language, which he rarely spoke. "I'll wake your brother."

In the dark, Jacob pulled on the clothes that were scattered around his bedroom floor. He lit a lamp and carried it into the hall. His father was running down the stairs, his arms bent as though he already were holding the horse's reins. Jacob had never seen him move so fast. Usually Abraham walked with the pace and dignity of a man on his way to church. Years before, when Jacob was a boy, his schoolmates used to tease him by mimicking his father's solemn strut. Now, to tease his brother, Hermann, who was two years younger and had just come back from medical school in Omaha, Jacob sometimes mimicked his father.

Instead of following Abraham down the stairs, Jacob went into his brother's room. Hermann was tying his tie. Jacob had not even put on a collar.

"Going to a party?" he asked.

Hermann did not answer.

"You put on a fresh shirt, too," Jacob said.

Hermann brushed past him and ran down the hall. Jacob dawdled. He went back to his own room to get his pipe, stopped on the stairs to stuff the pipe's bowl and light the tobacco, and, downstairs, rummaged on the cluttered shelf in the mudroom for a cap he had not worn in months. When he finally went outside, shivering in the wind, to the stable, he found the horse hitched and his father and brother in the buggy. Jacob climbed up beside them. Abraham snapped the reins. At the gate, they turned onto the road away from town.

"Where are we going?" Jacob asked.

Abraham did not answer.

Jacob looked questioningly at his brother, who shrugged.

In the moonlight, the land around them was the bluish white of porcelain and looked as fragile. Jacob stuck his pipe in his coat pocket and closed his eyes. He bobbed to the rocking of the buggy. After making an emergency visit to one of his patients at night, he sometimes dozed like this and let the horse find its way back by itself, something his father disapproved of and never did when he went out on night calls, no matter how tired he was. Once, while Jacob slept, his horse, sidetracked by whim or appetite, wandered off the road. Jacob woke in a prairie, no path in sight. Abraham said this proved how irresponsible Jacob had been; but for Jacob, the surprise of the vast distances when he'd expected to wake surrounded by the walls of the stable had been so pleasant he thought the episode proved how valuable it was occasionally to give up control.

When Abraham stopped the buggy, Jacob opened his eyes. Below them, in a bend of the Black River, was the abandoned Stutz farm, the house, barn and silo, shed, outhouse, and grove of ash trees making a continuous silhouette against moonlit water beyond. The previous spring, Stutz, a widower, had slit his son's throat with a scythe. A neighbor found him sprinkling the boy's blood on the newly plowed field. By the time Abraham and Jacob arrived, Stutz had committed suicide by impaling himself on his harrow. Jacob, who had been reading about fertility rites in James George Frazer's *The Golden Bough*, was intrigued by the ritual aspects of the murder and suicide. Abraham, who once had treated Stutz's son for mumps, knew how much Stutz had loved the boy and wondered what could have driven the farmer to such violence. All around the inside of the curved silo wall they'd found the mummified bodies of crucified rodents. Ever since then, people in the Black River Valley avoided the farm, which the bank was selling cheap.

"I'm going to buy it and start a clinic there for the treatment of mental disorders," Abraham told his sons. "I want you to help me."

ODD PEOPLE: 1884–1901

Chapter 2

Abraham had come to Galilee with his family a quarter of a century earlier, when the town was only two dozen wooden buildings, ranked along two avenues parallel to the railroad track, Avenue A and Avenue B, and three streets which intersected the avenues at right angles, First Street, Second Street, and Third Street. Beyond the town, unbroken to the horizon, was grass, which, pressed down by the wind, was silvery. Huge cumulus clouds, their bottoms so flat they seemed sheared with a scalpel, moved rapidly across the sky, casting a shadow which approached the town as fast as the train was leaving it. As the engine entered the shadow, the white plume from its funnel turned yellow and seemed to solidify.

Abraham took off his top hat and removed from the lining, where he'd kept it ever since leaving New York City, a brochure for Galilee, which optimistically mapped out a city of a hundred streets, printed in green, enough avenues, printed in red, to exhaust the alphabet, and nearly ten thousand building lots, numbered in blue. On the other side, an eagle with outspread wings grasped a banner in its talons.

GALILEE, the banner read, THE FUTURE OF AMERICA.

Abraham crumpled the brochure and tossed it onto the unpaved street. The breeze carried it a few hundred feet until it caught on the newly raised framework of a building, whose bare beams made it look like a huge picked-clean skeleton.

A little behind Abraham stood his wife, Rosa. When she was calm, she was not beautiful. The broadness of her forehead was exaggerated by how tightly she pulled back her hair, which she wore in a bun at the back of her head. Her nose, long and sharp, seemed an axis, on either side of which her features were arranged, as though an engineer had plotted her face on graph paper. And her chin, the engineer's principal blunder, was so large it seemed as though she'd been given a man's jaw. Grief, however, beautified her. When she wept, she pulled back her chin; and her face compressed itself, until all her features were brought into harmony. Having a vague sense of how lovely she looked when she was upset, she learned to distrust, not unhappiness, but beauty.

She held Hermann, who was then a toddler, in one arm. As she stared out at the bleak town, she rubbed her cheek against the top of his head, which made him twitch his eyelids in his sleep. With her other hand, she gripped Jacob, who was three, so tightly around the shoulders that he winced and tried to pry her fingers loose. She felt not just unhappy, but hurt, as though she were the butt of some horrible practical joke. When Abraham had suggested moving West, she'd imagined her future would somehow be like her past. She'd spent the first seven years of her life on a farm on Staten Island. In 1863, her father and mother had been murdered by rioters who, objecting to the draft, blamed it on the war, and the war on the blacks. Rosa's father, Gebhardt Luft, had a black hired hand, whom he hid in the hayloft. When the rioters tried to set fire to the barn, Gebhardt fought them off. Rosa, who watched the battle in the farmyard from an upstairs window of the house, did not understand what was happening. She recognized many of the rioters as neighbors. And because she'd never before seen her father angry, he seemed, dancing around brandishing a pitchfork in the flickering glare from the rioters' torches, to have been transformed into a devil. After he wounded one man in the arm, Gebhardt was stoned to death. Rosa's mother, Angelica, ran outside, waving her apron at the killers, who, terrified at their own violence, started throwing rocks at her, too. They retreated without having burned the barn.

The hired man crept out of his hiding place and later found Rosa, lying in her bed fully dressed, staring at the ceiling. He took her to Manhattan, to her uncle's house, which already was crowded with her twelve cousins. The cousins resented Rosa, since her presence meant their portions at meals would be smaller. Her aunt, unable to cope with the distractions of a large family, let her teenaged children run the house while she sat alone in her darkened bedroom, waiting for the spirits of her ancestors to rap on her lap table. She had trouble remembering the names of her own children, who she was sure were growing up and changing only to confuse her. Whenever she met Rosa on the stairs or in the hall, she suspiciously asked, "Are you one of mine?"

Rosa began to cultivate the memory of a picnic she'd gone on with her parents a few weeks before they were killed. In the memory, which idealized the day, they sat in a grove of pine trees on soft, dark green grass by a shallow brook in which tiny fish flashed like slivers of mirrors. As they ate, they smiled at each other, as though they shared some secret. In reality, the day had been overcast. Her father, who disliked picnics, ate quickly and, when he was through, hurried them back to the house. But she treasured her memory of that afternoon for years.

This was the past she confused with her future. In the months before moving to Nebraska, while the elevated train screamed outside the window of their four-room flat, Rosa went to sleep every night picturing her family —Abraham, Jacob, Hermann, and herself—picnicking in a grove of trees by a shallow stream near their new house in the West.

As they stood by the railroad tracks in Galilee, gazing at the barren little town, Rosa said, "I want to go home."

Gently putting his hand on the small of her back, Abraham said, "This is home."

Chapter 3

Home, during the first year of their life in Galilee, was three rooms behind the printer's shop. They slept in the smallest room, on beds Abraham had built from scrap lumber and old signs he got from the printer, who was also the town signmaker. Abraham did not bother to repaint the wood. The side of the children's bed read, in blue letters shaded with gold: BOOTS & SHOES, HATS & CAPS, LEDYARD T. BLANKENSHIP, DRYGOODS & CLOTHING. The side of Abraham and Rosa's bed read, upside down in black letters: FURLONG & DOUGLAS, REAL ESTATE, INSURANCE, AND LOAN AGENT. In designing the beds, Abraham had miscalculated. The children's was too high: Jacob, in trying to mount a nightmare, would tumble out, and Rosa was afraid Hermann, with a younger brother's self-destructive idolatry, would imitate Jacob. Abraham and Rosa's was too narrow. So Abraham slept with Jacob, and Rosa slept with Hermann.

The middle-size room, which served as both kitchen

and parlor, was so cramped Rosa had to cook on a diminutive wood stove; it had a crack, through which flames could be seen flickering when the stove was fired up. Abraham built a high chair for Hermann, who at first refused to try it because the bottom, made from an old meat market sign, had the horns of a steer on it. Since they had only two straight-back chairs, which Rosa and Jacob used, Abraham sat at the head of their small table in a rocker. He got into the habit of rocking forward to cut and fork up his food and rocking backward to chew it. For the rest of his life, no matter what kind of chair he sat on, he ate his meals rocking back and forth.

The largest room in the apartment, Abraham's office, was filled with furniture shipped from the East, the family's only luxury: a mahogany examination table; a screen embroidered with the battle of the *Monitor* and the *Merrimack*; a desk with a roll top that reminded Abraham of the segmented abdomen of certain beetles. The lamps were immaculate. Every morning he trimmed their wicks and washed their chimneys and green globes. On one side of his desk was a cabinet with glass doors above and wooden doors below. Abraham's scalpels, probes, tweezers, and saws were tucked into velvet-lined compartments of wooden boxes. A few other tools lay in a tray. Late in the afternoon, the low sun, reflecting off the blades, cast pale parallel rainbows on the opposite wall and ceiling. On the other side of the desk was another cabinet of similar design. The shelves were lined with blue, amber, and clear glass apothecary bottles, a pill press, a balance scale, and a mortar and pestle made of stone the color of cheese.

Behind the desk was a bookcase, its shelves packed with texts and journals, which Abraham subscribed to and which he read with admiration and envy. Most of the journals came from Germany, where Abraham wished he could study. The authors of the articles obviously worked with modern equipment, had access to up-to-date information, and, most important, betrayed none of the doubts about their own competence which Abraham felt. For Abraham, examining a patient was like feeling his way in the dark through a familiar room, parts of which had been vandalized, and trying blindly to assess the extent of the damage. Treatment often was limited to easing a patient's discomfort, raising his spirits, and keeping the family from starting to mourn while the patient was still alive.

Before Abraham came, when people in the Black River Valley were sick, they had no one to turn to except the druggist, Fritz Lorenz, an Austrian immigrant who had invested in land around Galilee and, along with two other speculators, had bribed the railroad to stop at the town. He bled his patients or purged them with calomel, or both. He prescribed opiates and patent medicines like Balm of Childhood, Ayer's Cathartic Pills, Dr. B. F. Sherman's Pricklyash Bitters, and Dr. Kilmer's Female Remedy, one of his most frequently recommended tonics, since so many of his patients were women. Men, for the most part, tended themselves, strapping splints on broken bones, using Indian remedies for chronic complaints like rheumatism, and sweating out fevers with liquor. And grandmothers jealously guarded their right to minister to sick children with traditional family cures, made from barks, roots, and berries, and often not that different from the Indian potions.

Lorenz had massive shoulders, which he curved forward to make them seem even more imposing; skin ridged like the bark of a locust tree; and hands large enough to completely cover a man's face. He also had a droopy mustache, which he sucked on when he was angry, combing it into his mouth with his bottom teeth. He resented Abraham's superior knowledge and skill, which he was afraid would lure patients away from him. He concocted a plan to humiliate Abraham so no one in town would respect him, respect being more vital to a doctor than training.

Lorenz owned a big dog, part German shepherd, part Newfoundland, and, according to town tradition, part timber wolf, famous for attacking anyone either ignorant or foolish enough to stray into the shed behind the drugstore, in which it was caged. Assuming correctly that Abraham had not yet heard of the dog, Lorenz sent his youngest boy, Bernard, to fetch him.

"Pa's sick bad in the shed," said Bernard, unable to repress a smirk. Instead of waiting to make sure the doctor came, Bernard surprised Abraham by bolting from the office. Abraham grabbed his bag and followed.

Bernard walked stiffly along the dusty street, arms straight down at his sides. Two men sauntered out of the general store and silently came down onto the street to walk slightly behind Abraham. Another man slipped out of the barbershop and also wandered up the street, a little apart from Abraham. A man who'd been sitting in a chair tilted back against a shop wall on the raised wooden sidewalk stood, letting his chair clatter upright, and joined the group. By the time Abraham reached the drugstore, half the men in town were with him. Lorenz had advertised his joke.

Bernard stopped next to the shed door.

"In there," he said, squinting at Abraham, his teeth bared in an effort to look innocent.

Abraham stared into Bernard's upturned face. Bernard glanced down. When Abraham unhooked the rope latch, Bernard backed away, and the men, who made a half circle around the front of the shed, leaned forward. Abraham opened the door and walked in.

The shed was hot and musty and stank so much he gagged. He stepped sideways away from the doorway. Sunlight made a trapezoid on the ground inside, the smaller end of which shone on two large brown paws. As Abraham's eyes got used to the gloom beyond the paws, he made out the biggest dog he'd ever seen, tensing for a leap. He swung his bag just as the dog sprang, hitting the animal on the side of the head. The dog landed and whirled. Abraham dropped his bag. When the dog jumped again, Abraham ducked under it and grabbed it around the neck, jamming his thumbs into its throat.

The dog swallowed against his thumbs, thrashed, snapped its teeth, and made a horrible gargling growl, which vibrated up Abraham's arms to his elbows. Twice it almost whipped itself free, but Abraham was strong and had learned how to hold on to writhing bodies while assisting in amputations in New York. As the dog died, Abraham sank to the ground with it, first on one knee and then on both knees. From behind, because of the spasms in his shoulders caused by the effort of throttling the dog, it looked as though he were sobbing.

When the dog was dead, Abraham stood. He glanced around for and found his hat, which had tumbled off during the fight; adjusted his coat; picked up his bag; and walked out into the sunlight, which bleached expression from the faces of the waiting men.

Bernard was gnawing on his lower lip.

Abraham said, "Tell your pa if he still feels poorly tomorrow to give me another call."

Chapter 4

The people of the Black River Valley agreed that any man who could kill Lorenz's dog with his bare hands could be trusted. The logic appalled Abraham, but he profited from the conclusion. The following day he was sitting at his desk, displeased because he'd just caught himself admiring the professional look of a note he'd written in the margin of one of his textbooks, when Rosa opened the door that led from his office into their parlor-kitchen.

"A man says his boy's sick," she announced, and stepped aside.

A farmer hesitated on the threshold. No matter how urgent his errand was, out of respect for the new doctor he'd taken the time to dress up. He was wearing what was obviously his best suit, heavy wool trousers and an equally heavy, although not quite matching, wool frock coat, which made him sweat terribly in the hot summer weather. He did not wear a hat, and his hair was so slicked down it had a dull sheen, like oilcloth. Just before entering, he must have been nervously touching his hair, because the hand he offered Abraham was greasy.

"I came in through the parlor," he said, "because I didn't want to disturb you."

"You're not disturbing me," Abraham said. "Your boy's my first patient here. What's wrong with him?"

"He's got the fever," the man said. "I can't pay you now."

"Don't worry about that," Abraham said. "Any other symptoms?"

"What?" the man asked.

"Can you tell me anything more about him?" Abraham asked.

"I thought it was the sun," he said. "Head aches. And he didn't eat. He kept saying his back hurt. He didn't want to work. But he's not lazy. He's always been a good boy. So I let him go. He's been in bed two weeks. The other doctor, Lorenz—"

"He's not a doctor," Abraham interrupted.

"He charges a dollar a visit," he said, "no matter where you live."

Abraham knew the man was lying. Lorenz charged an extra twenty-five cents for every mile beyond town he had to go.

"Don't worry about that," Abraham repeated.

"I won't give you more than a dollar," the man said.

"That's fine," Abraham said.

"And only if he gets better," he said.

"What's your name?" Abraham asked.

"Whittaker," the farmer said.

When Whittaker arrived, Abraham had judged him to be nearly fifty years old. Maybe older. His cheeks were caved in, and his features were as shriveled as the faces on the dried carved apples that Abraham's mother used to make for Christmas when Abraham was a boy. But

Whittaker's forehead was relatively smooth, and his big jug ears were young.

"How old are you, Mr. Whittaker?" Abraham asked.

"Thirty-two," Whittaker said, puzzled by the question.

"How long have you been out here?"

"Five years."

"Having a hard time?"

Whittaker laughed. "You think?" he asked back.

"I think yes, you are," Abraham said.

Whittaker looked at the open book on Abraham's desk. He licked his lower lip slowly from one corner of his mouth to the other and then glanced up, surprised by his own lapse of attention.

"It's my son who's sick, not me," he said.

But Abraham's questions had disarmed him. He had dropped his obsequious yet bullying manner.

"I'd appreciate it if you took a look at him," he said.

Whittaker owned one horse, a sick animal whose strength he wanted to save, so he'd walked the twelve miles into town. When others in the Black River Valley needed medical help, they hung up a bed sheet during the day or a lantern at night, a signal that was passed from farm to farm until it reached Galilee and Lorenz—and now Abraham—could be summoned. But Whittaker, jealous of how easy farming seemed for everyone else, did not get along with his neighbors and, misjudging them, assumed that they would not pass his message on. He also did not want to feel in debt to anybody, although, because his farm was doing so poorly, he frequently borrowed tools and supplies from the more affluent homesteads in the area, a private tax he levied and felt he deserved. The more he borrowed, the more he resented those who lent things to him, since he was sure people did so only to remind him of their success and his failure.

As they rode out to Whittaker's farm on Abraham's

buckboard, the two men for the most part kept to themselves. Occasionally Abraham asked a question, and Whittaker, his bluster and resentment gone, shyly answered. Whittaker was grateful for Abraham's concern, but afraid that Abraham's probing would uncover some uncouth secret that was hidden from everyone else—even himself, since he had no idea what the secret might be. He only knew that it had to exist, because he always felt guilty. Abraham found himself, as usual, distracted by the personality of the man who had sought his help. He was always getting sidetracked by his patients' stories, which was why he felt he was not a good doctor. He was confident that he knew his business, but often feared, when his patients recovered, that he'd flimflammed them into getting better, as though his interest in the patient and the patient's family had been as responsible for the cure as any of the medicines he'd prescribed. He had a knack for easing mental suffering simply by listening and caring. A minister's knack, he said to himself. He did not mean it as a compliment.

Whittaker's farmhouse was a sod hut built into the side of a hill. The fence around a pen was broken in half a dozen places. On the windmill, two sails were missing, making the machine look like a half-plucked daisy. And Whittaker's horse, very black against the cloudless sky, its ears curving from its head like horns, was as gaunt as Whittaker.

"Don't you have any other children to help you with the place?" Abraham asked.

"Two girls and another boy died," Whittaker said. He quickly added, "but that was a long time ago and they were very young."

Abraham climbed down from the buckboard. Whittaker ran to pull open the door of the sod hut. Four broken wooden steps led down into the dim room, which smelled of earth. Two chimney holes in the roof let in light. There were no windows. Abraham felt as though he were descending into a grave.

"You've kept the boy down here?" he asked. To soften the disapproving sharpness of the question, he added, "Where is he?"

Whittaker gestured toward a corner.

"Could I have a light?" Abraham asked.

"We don't have much kerosene," Whittaker said.

Abraham felt his way across the room. He banged his shin against a stool.

In the corner, serving as a bed, was a large sled. On a thin mat of straw lay someone who—Abraham could just make out—was sucking on a thumb like a baby. That was the source of the kissing sound Abraham had heard ever since entering. He bent closer, and was just about to tell Whittaker that at least his son seemed active, a promising sign—although the activity was somewhat odd for a ten-year-old—when he realized the figure sucking its thumb was a woman, Whittaker's wife.

Abraham flung back the blanket. Cramped between Whittaker's wife and the wall was a small thin child, more the size of a six- than a ten-year-old, and seeming smaller yet in an oversized nightshirt. Abraham touched the boy's forehead.

"Wrap him in the blanket and help me carry him outside," Abraham told Whittaker.

Even when they bent down to pick up the boy, Whittaker's wife did not stop sucking her thumb. The sound was bestial. When they got outside, Abraham could not remember if the woman's eyes had been open or closed.

Once they were in the light, Whittaker said, "I can handle him myself now."

Abraham could not tell if this possessiveness sprang from Whittaker's distrust of him or from a desire to hug the frail body, which he held upright against his chest as though he were burping a baby.

From love, Abraham decided as he watched Whittaker's free hand stroking the boy's back.

Carefully, Whittaker laid the child under the buckboard, the only shade. The boy's lips were covered with a crust that looked like the brown scum on burned milk. Abraham raised the nightshirt and examined the boy's abdomen and chest. The nightshirt was stained in back.

"Diarrhea?" he asked Whittaker. Abraham stripped the boy and tossed the dirty nightshirt on the ground. "Do you have any clean clothes?" he asked.

Whittaker disappeared into the house and returned with a pair of not particularly clean long johns.

"Anything else?" Abraham asked.

Whittaker muttered something.

"What?" Abraham asked.

"My wife hasn't had a chance to do the wash for a while," Whittaker said.

"Do the wash," Abraham told Whittaker. He poked the soiled nightshirt with the toe of his boot. "This, the sheets, everything. Where do you keep your food?"

Whittaker started on a long, defensive explanation, which Abraham only half heard, because his attention was distracted by Whittaker's wife, who was standing in the doorway, the wooden frame cutting her off at the waist so she looked like a hand puppet. She stared at them for a while and then ducked out of sight.

Hopeless, Abraham thought.

"Is your water supply good?" he asked, interrupting Whittaker, who had strayed into an attack on a neighbor who all winter and spring had brought baskets of food for them.

"If the pump worked right," said Whittaker, angrily pointing at the windmill, as though its failure to function properly were its own fault. "There's good water down there. This is fine land. A fine farm, could be a fine one, if the boy hadn't come down sick. We were in the fields working when it happened. We'd be far along now, far along. Wouldn't need anyone's charity."

"Get me a bucket of water," said Abraham.

The boy's lips started moving, but no sound came out. Abraham took off his coat, which was as heavy as Whittaker's, although of better quality, and rolled up his shirt sleeves. When Whittaker brought the water, Abraham soaked his handkerchief, wrung it out, and began wiping the boy with the damp cloth to bring down the fever.

"Could you fix up a tent or lean-to?" Abraham asked Whittaker.

Whittaker started to explain how he intended to build a wooden house. Abraham said, "Quickly, please."

For two hours, Abraham bathed the boy. Four times he called Whittaker over to get fresh water. Each time, Whittaker, glad for the excuse to take a rest, hung around the buckboard until Abraham told him to get back to work. The boy's fever went down. He stopped moving his lips. Abraham dressed him in the long johns and, leaving him in the buckboard's shadow, helped Whittaker finish building the lean-to, which, when done, was not very strong or elaborate, but offered protection from the sun and wind, and was certainly better for the boy than the pestilential hole in which he'd been living. While Whittaker dragged the sled to the lean-to, Abraham cut fresh grass for the mattress with Whittaker's dull scythe. After bedding the boy down, Abraham built a fire outdoors and set a tub on it to boil water. As Whittaker washed the pitifully small load of laundry, Abraham sat on the grass and explained about bathing the boy to bring down the fever.

"What's wrong with him?" Whittaker asked without looking up from the washtub.

"Typhoid," Abraham said.

Whittaker stopped stirring the clothes with a stick.

"What's his name?" Abraham asked quickly.

"Joseph," Whittaker said.

"What's your wife's name?" Abraham asked.

"Evelyn," Whittaker said. He started stirring the clothes again.

"How long has she been like this?"

"Like what?" Whittaker asked. He levered a soggy gray mass out of the steaming water. It slipped off the end of the stick and plopped back into the tub. "Nothing's wrong with her."

Abraham poked his head into the lean-to. Joseph was sleeping calmly. A fly was walking across his sweating forehead. Abraham brushed it away. It spiraled up into the air and settled again on the boy's forehead. Joseph murmured in his sleep and turned his head. The fly flew off.

In the sod house, Evelyn sat, a shadow at a shadowy table. Abraham found a wobbly chair and sat across from her.

"I think your boy will be all right," he said.

"He's fine," she said. Her voice cracked. She hadn't spoken for a long time.

"No," Abraham said. "He's very sick, but he should get better if you tend him properly. Do you think you can do that?"

"He's strong and healthy," she said.

"He needs you to take care of him," Abraham said.

"I had three other children," she said. "Lincoln, Bettina, and Rachel." At each name, she tapped the table with her forefinger.

"Tell me about them," Abraham said.

For an hour, Evelyn talked—or rather sang, because she had a way of sending her sentences up and down the scale. It sounded musical and, since it put emphasis in places that made no sense, hysterical. Mostly she described clothes she'd made or wished she could have made for the dead children. Her mother had been a seamstress, and so was she.

"I'm good," she said, her voice dead level, no fluting up and down the scale now. A challenge as well as a boast.

Abraham exploited the moment.

"How come you don't do any sewing for town, then?" he asked.

There was a long pause. Abraham was afraid he'd made a mistake and driven her back into herself.

"I could," she said at last.

"I have two children, one and three," Abraham said. "Would you make nightshirts for them?"

When she hesitated, he added, "I'll supply the cloth."

"I don't have any needles," she said.

"And needles, thread, whatever else you need," Abraham said. "And, while you're at it, make one for your son, too."

"He won't die?" she asked.

Abraham was pleased she no longer pretended he was well.

"I don't know," he said. "I don't think so."

Outside, washed clothes lay drying on the grass. Whittaker crouched in the lean-to, wiping his son's forehead with a damp rag. Abraham joined him.

"I'll stop by tomorrow," he said. As they walked to the buckboard, he added, "Your wife's going to make my children nightshirts. That'll settle our debt."

Whittaker glanced suspiciously at Abraham.

"Do you think that's too much?" Abraham asked, surprised.

"Yes," Whittaker said.

"If they're good, maybe I'll buy some others," Abraham said.

Whittaker grunted.

Abraham climbed onto his buckboard, nodded to Whittaker, and shook the reins.

A long winter, Abraham thought. Long winters and isolation affect people in strange ways.

For a month, he visited three times a week, spending more time with them than he should have, but their progress pleased him. The Whittakers were among his few successes. Then, because he was busy with other cases, he didn't go to their farm for a month and a half. When he did, he found it deserted. The door of the sod hut was ajar. The lean-to had collapsed. At the depot, he learned they had returned East. Abraham was annoyed they hadn't said good-bye, but he was happy he'd helped them—and not just medically. The Whittakers left Abraham with a new respect for his minister's knack.

Chapter 5

Over the years, Abraham became known as the Talking Doctor—paradoxically, since he listened more than he talked; but after rambling on to him, people were left with the impression that he'd given them good advice or had explained things that previously had defied their understanding. Having tended his patient, Abraham would sit for hours with the patient's family, who would try to entertain him in the parlor, formally. But Abraham preferred sitting with them in the kitchen. Abraham found that in the relaxed atmosphere of the kitchen people betrayed their oddities. And he became convinced that everyone was odd.

"Doesn't that sound bother you?" one woman asked as they sat before the fireplace.

Abraham had just opened an abscess on her son's arm, and the boy was sleeping peacefully upstairs in his bed.

"What sound?" Abraham wondered.

"Why," the woman said, "the sound of the house settling."

Abraham listened. All he heard was the fire, the ticking of a clock in the next room, and the creak of the rocker in which the woman sat.

"It's so loud," she said, "I can't go to sleep nights."

Another woman, who was doing laundry as she talked to Abraham, folded each item at least three times, trying to make sure the corners were aligned exactly. A man, whose daughter Abraham was treating for measles, used a straight razor to trim the strands of tobacco that hung over the edge of his pipe bowl. He explained, "I like a neat smoke."

There were tappers, people who had to touch something—like a watch chain—a number of times before continuing with whatever they were doing. There were cleaners, people who scrubbed things over and over, when one good wash would have been sufficient. And there were those with nervous tics, hiccups, and laughs. What struck Abraham as most bizarre of all was that no one thought their own quirks odd. When he would ask people about their curious habits, they'd deny they did what he claimed or explain that they did nothing different from anyone else—everyone felt the same way about the sound of a settling building or the importance of a neat smoke.

At first Abraham found this strange behavior funny and sad. Once their eccentricities were revealed, people seemed vulnerable. Abraham wanted to hug them, because they were pathetic, because they were comic, because they were unique. But little by little he began to feel oppressed by this clarity of vision, which not only allowed but compelled him to see the oddness in people. Finally, this compulsion horrified him. He was like a man at a costume party, who starts by being amused at the fantastic masks his companions are wearing and ends by understanding that the masks are, in fact, his companions' faces. The party is not a party; it is his life.

Abraham realized that he, too, was odd: he'd become obsessed with oddness.

One evening, as he sat before the fire, he found himself making up a story out of the shapes he saw in the flames. He decided to keep a record of his fire fantasies. He found a notebook, sat back down, and tried to impose order on the flickering images, but the faces, towers, and landscapes dissolved under his attention until all that remained was the fire. The more he strained, the more stubborn the fire became. Angry, he tossed the notebook into the fireplace. A page curled as it burned, as though the fire itself were reading the book. Abraham's mind wandered. As page after page caught and curled, he read in the burning book a dreamlike story.

He jumped up. This was the way to catch those images —by not concentrating. Sitting at his desk, he jotted down as much as he could recall of his reverie.

From then on, every night, before going to bed, he dreamed in front of the fire and wrote out the fragments that stayed with him. He was not sure what to do with the gibberish he recorded, but there were enough familiar faces and places in the flames for him to suspect that the fire, or rather he himself through the fire, was speaking in code—a code he'd invented to hide from himself what he wanted to tell himself. All he had to do was find a way of cracking the code.

He made lists of recognizable images and of images which, although unrecognizable, were repeated night after night. Certain ones, like a garden with a high hedge, seemed to be important. Whenever he noticed these repeating images, his breathing and heartbeat quickened.

Why they had such an intense effect on him remained a mystery.

In his visits with his patients' families, he asked them what they saw in the fireplace flames or, if it was summer, in the billowing folds of their curtains. One woman described the eyes and forehead of her dead son. A man described a system of flywheels and belts on his steam thresher. Another man described his father's hat, which had in its hatband a feather his father never wore. Some people saw certain recurring pictures, which, like Abraham's garden, became more and more elaborate with every appearance—or which changed over a number of appearances. A rope swing turned into a ladder. An upright piano turned into a brass bedstead. One woman, whose right arm became paralyzed after she had cradled her dying husband in it, saw in the flames her hair, which people had admired ever since she was a child.

"It's tangled," she said. "Snarled. I haven't brushed it in days. It's dirty. I'm sure it smells."

She reached up with the hand that was supposed to be paralyzed and brushed back her hair.

"You moved your arm," Abraham said.

"When?" the woman asked.

"Just now."

"I'm sure you're mistaken," the woman said. "I can't move my arm.

He filled page after page of large green-covered ledgers with anecdotes about his patients and their families. But anecdotes were all his descriptions were. They simply recounted day by day what Abraham saw. He wanted to do more than just report how people behaved. He wanted to make sense of it. He tried organizing his anecdotes in various ways. The odd things people with the same disease did. The odd things people who lived in sod houses did compared to the odd things people who lived in more comfortable circumstances did. The odd things people in town did compared to the odd things people on farms did. The odd things women did compared to the odd things men did. Children below ten; children above ten. Pregnant women; barren women. Men with families; bachelors. Drunkards; teetotalers. Those who believed women should get the vote; those who did not. Members of one family; members of another family.

It was easy enough to trace patterns. But Abraham had no idea what the patterns meant. Why all the Mendenhalls—father, mother, grandmother, and six children—shared the same delusion that every night, after everyone went to sleep, a dog padded through their house sniffing at each bedroom door in turn. They did not own a dog. Their doors and windows were locked. The dog could not exist. But the family matter-of-factly agreed it did. They no longer were curious about where it came from. They accepted it, a nocturnal mystery pet. Why?

Abraham's interest in bizarre behavior turned into impatience.

"It's all gossip," he told Rosa. "I'm wasting my time."

He locked his ledgers in his desk and tried to concentrate on his routine medical practice. Although he continued to notice—could not help noticing—bizarre behavior, he took no more notes until he wrote for himself a detailed account of what happened to Helen Blankenship. His first case history.

Helen Blankenship, the daughter of Galilee's mayor, was two years old when Abraham met her. She toddled to a chair, picked up a closed book her father had left there, and tugged on the bookmark.

"Don't pull that out," her father said.

"Don't pull that out," she repeated to herself, more sharply than her father had said it.

Then she pulled out the bookmark. She looked from the book, which she held in one hand, to the bookmark in the other and burst into tears. When her father picked her up to calm her, she bit his cheek so hard she broke the skin. Blankenship sent his wife to get Abraham, who arrived to find Helen sitting quietly on the sofa, destroying a stalk of decorative pampas grass. When he started cleaning the two bleeding crescent-shaped wounds on Blankenship's cheek, he glanced at Helen and asked, "Are you the little girl with the big bite?"

She smiled fiercely, showing her teeth.

"Little wolf," she said.

Wolf was right. Fourteen years later, in 1898, the night after her sixteenth birthday, she sneaked out of her bedroom and ran through the neighborhood, naked on all fours. Abraham, walking home from a house call, saw Helen dashing through an empty lot, her body pale, lithe, shockingly lovely in the moonlight.

"Helen," he called.

She stopped and looked at him over her shoulder. She was panting, her mouth open and tongue hanging out. When Abraham called a second time, she stood and walked to him as naturally as if she were dressed and it were two in the afternoon instead of two in the morning.

"Will you take me home?" she asked.

The next day, as her family hovered inside the house, Helen lounged in the backyard in a hammock. As she swung, she talked to Abraham, who sat in a straight-back chair.

"Do you remember what happened last night?" he asked.

"I should say no," she said, "shouldn't I?"

Abraham smiled.

"I don't remember leaving the house," she said. "But I remember running with the wind all over my body. I was so light. I weighed nothing at all."

She frowned. Abraham followed her gaze across the lawn. In a kitchen window, her father's face floated in the shadows. Helen kicked the ground and sent the hammock flying.

Every afternoon that summer, Abraham visited Helen. He asked her to tell him what she saw in the clouds and in the moving shadows of leaves. She swung in the hammock or walked across the lawn or sat on the Blankenships' wide front porch and talked and talked.

"It's not proper," said Mrs. Blankenship one day, after telling Abraham that Helen was in her room and could not come down. She was a short, plump woman with a braid of hair curled on her head. "It's like you're courting her."

"Not that we think you are," Blankenship assured him.

"But it doesn't look right," she said. "So the boys don't come around. She should be seeing people her own age."

"What she did that time," Blankenship said, "it was a prank. You're taking it too seriously."

"She's a good girl," Mrs. Blankenship said. "High-spirited is all."

After his wife left, Blankenship raised his eyebrows in apology.

"I know you're trying to help," he said. "But I don't understand what all that talk can do. And I've heard once or twice through the window . . ." He caught himself. "When I was just passing. She's telling you things it isn't right for her to say."

"I want to keep seeing her," Abraham said.

"You can't," Blankenship said.

"I want to keep seeing her," Abraham repeated.

"Why is it so important?" Blankenship asked.

"I don't know," Abraham said.

"Then how am I supposed to say yes?"

"Do you trust me?"

Blankenship spread out his arms, an ambiguous gesture.

As Abraham turned to go, Blankenship called after him, a final plea for understanding: "She's my daughter."

Early that autumn, Helen again ran naked through the town. Blankenship's oldest son, William, heard her slam the front door. He and his father went after her. They chased her for over a mile and, having caught her, carried her home like a shot beast, Blankenship holding her ankles and his son holding her arms, a coat draped over her body. The next night, Blankenship locked her bedroom door. She escaped through the window, dropping two flights and hobbling off on a sprained ankle. The night after that, Blankenship tied her to her bed. She struggled in the ropes for hours, until she'd rubbed both wrists raw. Finally, she freed one hand, untied herself, and, finding the windows nailed shut, plunged through the glass. By the time Abraham got there, she was dead. She'd been cut so badly in so many places that, lying in the darkened room on her bed, the blood drying in streaks all over her body, she looked as though she were changing into not a wolf but a tiger.

"Could you have helped her?" Blankenship asked.

"I wish I knew," Abraham said.

Abraham read everything he could find on psychopathology. The journals and texts stacked on the floor turned his office into a maze through which patients had to wander to reach him. He would listen to their complaints, treat them, and return to his reading. The current explanations of mental illness, which held heredity, hormonal imbalance, brain damage, or diseases of the nervous system responsible, frustrated him. If mental illness were organic in origin, he was stymied. Medicine might someday find cures, as it might for other diseases, but in the meantime what could he do? Although listening helped, it was not enough. His presence could calm the distraught, but he could not stay around the clock with someone who was upset.

"You've changed," Rosa said one night.

They were in their new house, which had twelve rooms and was decorated on the outside with so much fretwork—circles, diamonds, miniature Moorish arches, and fleurs-de-lis—that it looked like something from a fairy tale. From their bedroom window Rosa could see their immaculate lawn, the curved drive leading to the stable, and their picket fence, white as bone under the full moon.

The night was still and hot. She fanned herself with her hand as she walked to the bed, a four-poster shipped from Albany, and sat on the side. Age had softened her features, as grief used to. Only her mouth, which was straight, turning neither up nor down at the ends, retained the hardness of her youth.

"I was watching you across the table tonight," she told Abraham, "and I realized you don't laugh anymore."

"Did I ever?" Abraham asked.

"You used to laugh all the time."

"I suppose," he said, "everything used to seem funny."

"And now?" she asked.

"Puzzling," he said, climbing forward into bed and walking across the mattress on his knees like a child, instead of backing into bed, sitting on the mattress, and swinging his legs up like an adult.

"Are they so fascinating?" she asked.

"Who?" Abraham asked.

"Everybody else," she said.

"I can't neglect my patients," he said.

Watching the regular motion of Rosa's arm as she dragged the brush through her hair was making Abraham sleepy. He let his eyes close.

"What do you expect to learn from them?" she asked.

Her voice came from a long way off. He was caught in the undertow of sleep and was being carried away. His answer seemed disembodied, as far from him as her question had been. He said, "Why people do what they do."

Chapter 6

Jacob and Hermann did not escape their father's growing obsession. At night Abraham sat in a chair at the foot of their beds, his shadow monstrous on the wall behind them, and instead of bedtime stories recited case histories.

In his monotonous voice, Abraham told of the Vampire of Dedham, a telegraph operator who was found drinking dog's blood; the Mole Woman of Sulphur Springs, whose brother had kept her locked in a closet for thirty years, who when Abraham discovered her was a pale, nearly blind, childlike creature in a dirty shift, mumbling gibberish which her brother insisted was Italian; and the Bloody Barber of Indian Orchard, who one day inexplicably sliced off a cheek of one of his customers. The cheek, which still had stubble on it, looked—people claimed—like a scrub brush.

Jacob did not like his father's stories. Every chance he had—early in the morning before anyone else was awake, after school, and late at night—he crept up to the attic and read fairy tales, legends, and mythology, books that his mother gave him and that Abraham forbade him to read.

"I want him to know the truth of things," he told Rosa. "Reality is strange enough. He doesn't need fantasies."

Psyche gazed into a forest pool, one breast bared. Andromache was chained to a rock, clad in transparent gauze. Guinevere wore a girdle that hung low on her belly; from it a sash dangled between her legs. Cinderella, in rags, showed quite a bit of leg. Jacob fell in love with first one then another of these women, his sexual feelings for them inextricable from his romantic longings. They represented a charmed world he yearned to enter. Their eroticism seemed as innocent as his response to it seemed corrupt. He believed that he was duping his mother into giving him these books and that his father was right to distrust them —although for reasons opposite those which his father gave. Jacob responded not to the fantasy in the stories, but to the reality that flashed through them.

This truth was as grim as any his father wanted to teach with his case histories. The fairy tales, legends, and myths were full of greed, revenge, passion, hate, thwarted expectations, hope outwitted by fate, pride . . . Pride especially. It was pride that appealed to Jacob most—his hero was Prometheus—because pride so often led to rebellion, and Jacob was by nature a rebel. Only by challenging what seemed to be could he learn what truly was. In resisting his father, he was following his father's lead. He wanted to know "the truth of things."

In the winter of 1897, when Jacob was fifteen years old, some people, first in Hastings, Nebraska, then in Inavale, Omaha, North Platte, Kearney, Grand Island, and Black River Junction, reported seeing an airship. The Galilee *Independent* ran a banner headline, SIGHTS IN THE SKY, in type as large as that used a few months before for BRYAN DEFEATED. The article, written in the enthusiastic and cynical style of a circus poster, described "this mysterious wonder of the modern world" as being nearly forty feet long, with wings fore and aft and a curved fin or rudder at its tail—"an impossible design," said a Galilee inventor, Richard Lingard, who had built his own flying machine, a pedal-powered helicopter, which had sixteen disks arranged along four wings. It looked like a flying harrow—something to plow clouds with—and did not fly. Lingard, a young man with a politician's smile and angry eyes, carted the machine from town to town in a horse-drawn wagon, drummed up a crowd, collecting a dime from each adult and a nickel from each child, and, folding back the canvas that hid his invention, pointed with an oak walking stick to each part and explained why the craft should have worked.

Abraham, in a rare mood, came to the dinner table reading the item aloud and rolling his eyes.

"Obviously, he's jealous," Rosa said.

"Obviously?" he asked his wife. "Do you think the good people of Nebraska are actually being visited by this—let's see, what does our correspondent call it—'ark from the heavens'? Are we all about to be saved from the disaster of ten-cents-a-bushel corn and carried off to a better land with bumper crops and higher prices?"

"You don't believe the reports?" Rosa asked.

"It says here," he said, "Thomas Edison claims it's nonsense."

"And you?"

"My dear," he said—he hardly ever addressed his wife as *my dear*—"a quarter of a century before we came here people were reporting flying snakes. Do you think snakes actually flew? I'm sure people believed they did, as I'm sure people believe they saw an airship."

"More odd behavior for you files," she said.

"The odd thing," he said, "is that so many people share the same delusion. And that their accounts are so detailed. Listen to this."

He read an interview with a farmer named Sylvester, who claimed that while he was shoveling a path from his house to his barn, the airship flew so low over him he could hear laughter and the chime of glasses being rung against each other in toasts.

"No doubt the airmen were congratulating each other on startling the rubes," Abraham said.

Rosa blushed.

That night, Jacob heard footsteps padding down the stairs. He slipped from bed and, holding his nightshirt close to protect himself from drafts, sneaked out of his room. Candlelight flickered in the stairwell and dimmed as whoever was carrying the candle moved from the front hall into the kitchen. After a short silence, he heard whoever it was stamping first one and then the other foot into boots.

Jacob dressed quickly, all the while glancing out his window, from which he could see the back door. The moon, which had just cleared the roofs of the houses, was huge. Its paleness made it seem as transparent as a paper lantern. Its light cast long thin shadows. The newly fallen snow was as glossy as satin. A figure—it must have been his mother, since it was bundled in his mother's navy blue overcoat—tromped, high-stepping through the deep drifts.

Jacob hurried downstairs, leaning on the banister so the treads would not creak under his weight. Outside, the air was so cold that every time he took a breath it felt as though a razor was shoved down his throat. He breathed through a mittened hand, but his breath condensed on the wool and froze to his lips. A strip across his forehead, a crescent on each cheek, the tips of his ears, and a dime-sized spot on his chin throbbed and grew numb. He was afraid his eyes would ice over the way the wash water did in his bedroom pitcher, and he imagined rapping his pupils with his forefinger to shatter the crust.

He followed his mother's trail. Under his feet, the snow she had packed down squeaked as distinctly and regularly as if he were walking on a path of white mice—an image he enjoyed since it made this adventure more like something out of a fairy tale. His shadow, gliding beside him, sitting up when it reached the snowbanks and lying flat again when it returned to level ground, was the kind of uncanny mute companion a fairy-tale hero would have on a quest. When Jacob turned onto Avenue M, a wide street guarded by stone lions crouched on pedestals, he found that his mother's track joined dozens of others. As Jacob approached the edge of town, he saw a red glow in the sky.

He rounded another corner and came upon a crowd of almost fifty people, half of whom carried torches. Illuminated from above, their faces looked ghoulish. No one spoke, eerie in so large a crowd. The wind sprang up. Snow puffed high into the air, glittering in the torchlight. People tucked in their chins and hunched their backs against the breeze.

In the center of the rough circle formed by this crowd was a large undulating shape, which reminded Jacob of the head of an octopus. As he watched, it grew from the size of a hay wagon to the size of a house. A balloon. Jacob sidled through the crowd to get a better look at the men who were tending the fire which was filling the balloon with hot air.

An airship party, Jacob thought.

The newspaper had described such gatherings in Omaha and Black River Junction, mobs of believers who met to search the skies for the airship, but he had never expected to find a group in Galilee. And his mother was one of the believers. He remembered how hurt she'd been at his father's crack about rubes earlier that night.

Jacob gazed around the crowd, trying to spot her. He knew everyone here: Ricky Furlong, a classmate; Bernard Lorenz, who now was twenty-one years old and a railroad agent; Chance Allen, the barber; fewer women than men, fewer children than women. No one acknowledged his greetings. It was as though all were participating in some unsavory rite, part of a secret life that was kept separate from the everyday world they shared.

Drunk on the oddness of the situation, Jacob leaned against one of the balloon's ropes. His attention drifted. Low voices blended into a hypnotic hum. He was thinking about his shadow gliding along the snow, faster and faster; he had to run to keep up with it; he'd become his shadow's shadow. He was out of breath; he couldn't run anymore; his shadow was about to leave him behind; he stumbled, and grabbed something to keep from falling. Something yanked his arm.

He opened his eyes. He'd stumbled in his dream as the balloon lifted off. To keep from falling he'd grabbed the rope, which he now held with both hands. The balloon dragged him for twenty feet before it rose. People around him—below him; the balloon was rising fast—shouted. He saw each face he sailed above with unnatural clarity. His mother's face beneath him—upturned, mouth open, teeth enameled red by the torchlight—seemed as comforting as it used to when it hovered above him as she tucked him into bed. Part of him still felt dreamy and enjoyed the sensation of flying, the way everything on the ground quickly became miniaturized; part of him realized he had only seconds to release the rope and drop, before the balloon rose so high that dropping would be death. As though someone slammed his hands with a mallet, his fingers started to hurt. Up to then he had not been aware of them. When he let go, one glove slipped off, frozen to the rope. He fell from what seemed a great height, although it was no more than fifteen feet, and landed in a snowbank, on his back.

Stars wheeled through the sky above him, stopped, and shrank back into their appointed places. The wind sounded like someone whistling through his teeth. The balloon must have carried him far from the crowd.

Grunting, he rolled over, got up on one knee, stood. He dug the snow from his pants legs and sleeves. On the trek home, his ungloved hand ached in his pocket.

Rosa was waiting for him in the kitchen. She'd changed into her nightgown and heavy brown bathrobe. Under her nightcap, her hair was down. There was a fire in the stove and a pot of milk warming. Jacob glanced at the clock. It was past four-thirty. He must have lain in the snowbank for a long time.

"Are you all right?" she asked.

Jacob nodded.

"Get into some dry clothes," she said. "I'll make some cocoa."

Neither that night nor at any time afterward did either of them mention her presence or his adventure at the airship party.

Chapter 7

For Rosa, dessert was the Orient of the dinner table, and she usually prepared something exotic. As a result, the Gottenbergs rarely had an ordinary dish like green apple pie—Hermann's favorite. One autumn afternoon, Hermann was sitting on the back steps, trying to whistle through a blade of grass stretched between his thumbs, when he smelled baking apples, cinnamon, and cloves. Apple pie! He ran to tell Jacob, who was reading, cross-legged, under a box elder.

"I'll wrestle you for dessert," said Jacob, putting down his book. "If I win, I'll get yours. But if you win, you'll get mine."

Before he wrestled with Jacob, Hermann had to wrestle with himself. The possibility of having no dessert alarmed him almost as much as the possibility of having two desserts tempted him.

Seeing Hermann hesitate, Jacob said, "For half your dessert?"

"No," Hermann said, "for all."

Jacob stood. They rushed at each other like rams. Jacob's right shoulder slammed into Hermann's They grabbed each other around the back of the neck. Locked together, they staggered across the field, slowly turning, until Hermann's legs buckled and he went down with Jacob on top of him. Hermann braced a foot behind himself and pushed. Jacob slammed him back to the ground. Frustrated, Hermann started weeping. Suddenly, Jacob went limp. Hermann spun free and lunged back, catching Jacob's neck in the crook of his arm.

"You win," Jacob said, gently tugging at his brother's grip.

They rolled away from each other and lay on their backs, gazing up at the mackerel sky. The clouds looked like curdled milk.

"You let me win," Hermann said.

That evening, he ate both his and Jacob's slices of pie, but he was so angry he could not concentrate on the taste. When he finished, he felt as cheated as if he'd lost the match.

Shortly after New Year's, the brothers again fought, this time in an empty lot near the school. The drifts were high. The boys plunged into the snow and came up gasping. Their sweaty faces steamed. Their freezing hair felt like pine needles. Jacob ended up on top. Underneath, Hermann wrenched himself back and forth. When Jacob suddenly loosened his grip, Hermann, not wanting to be tricked, stayed where he was, faking a struggle to escape. Jacob whispered, "All right," and rocked up until he pinned Hermann's shoulders. Hermann arched his back. Jacob pressed down harder on Hermann with his chest. Hermann writhed onto one side. Jacob forced him down. Hermann twisted to the other side just as Jacob relaxed his hold. Hermann's momentum carried him out and over. Jacob, now underneath, said, "You win."

"I will," Hermann said.

He took Jacob's head as tenderly as he might have held a child. Jacob smiled. Hermann smiled back and bashed his brother's skull against the ground. The tramped-down snow cushioned the blows enough to prevent serious injury, but not pain. Jacob roared and unsuccessfully struggled to buck Hermann off. From then on, when they wrestled, Jacob, like Hermann, fought to win.

That winter Jacob recognized Hermann as an equal not just in fights but also in companionship. He introduced him to fairy tales, legends, and mythology.

But Hermann wasn't interested. He returned Jacob's books, puzzled about what attractions they held for his brother. Only one story excited him: that of Prometheus—but while Jacob identified with the pride that drove Prometheus to steal fire from the gods, Hermann identified with the self-sacrifice that led him to give it to humankind. Hermann even envied Prometheus the eagle gnawing at his liver, because it was this suffering, the punishment for the crime, which raised the act to nobility.

Hermann took his cue from Prometheus. Education became theft, although it was not the teachers he had to steal from. He thought they were as ignorant as he was. It was life itself he wanted to rob of its secrets. He walked through the world, a burglar in a mansion, pocketing everything that caught his fancy. He turned a corner of the attic into a museum. His butterflies, moths, and beetles were preserved in glass-topped cases, which he propped along the baseboard, a dead army in review. He pressed leaves and flowers in books. The pages took on ghostly imprints, as though the paper had absorbed the plants' souls. Rocks, each with a spot of white paint in which a labeling number was inked, he stored in the four drawers of an old maple silverware cabinet Rosa gave him. He kept his two fossils, a three-toed footprint and a snail, in a special box he had built himself. He lined up his birds' eggs along the windowsill, each balanced on a wooden ring. And he tacked to the wall a map he'd drawn of the Black River Valley, on which he noted where and when he'd found each butterfly, moth, beetle, leaf, flower, rock, fossil, and egg.

"You can't be serious about so many subjects," said Abraham, who saw in this passion for collecting an obsession, which was unscientific.

Hermann shrugged.

"At least," Abraham said, "show me what you've done."

Hermann shook his head, no.

"Why not?" Abraham asked. "What are you hiding up there?"

Hermann's collections were not important in themselves. He brought home insects, plants, and rocks not because he had a naturalist's curiosity, but because they were evidence of his own capacity for wonder. Like a traveler in a strange land, he gathered his specimens less out of an interest in where he was than to prove he'd been there at all. What he was trying to steal from life was the secret of Hermann Gottenberg. What he was hiding in the attic was himself.

Once, before his sons were home from school, Abraham climbed the stairs into the attic. It was a spring day. The hot attic was filled with the sweet smell of aging wood.

He squatted first in Jacob's corner, then in Hermann's, trying to recall what had made the private corner he'd had as a child so comforting. It too had been by a window, as though these childhood nooks were as much vantage points as retreats. But his had not been as luxurious as his sons', just a cramped space between bed and cupboard that stank of mouse droppings, a corner separated only in his imagination from the rest of the single room in which he lived with his father, mother, and younger brother when they first came to New York City, in the mid-1860s.

Abraham carried one of Hermann's glass-topped cases to the window for better light. As he examined the insects, he became aware that he was being watched. Outside in the yard, gazing up at him, was Hermann. As Abraham raised a hand to wave, Hermann vanished into the house. Abraham leaned the case back against the wall and went downstairs. Hermann was gone, his schoolbooks left on the kitchen table.

That night, when Abraham went for an after-dinner walk, he found all Hermann's collections—the glass-topped cases shattered, the birds' eggs cracked, the leaf books and rock cabinet spilling their contents—dumped in the trash behind the stable.

A month and a half later, Hermann stole a ledger from his father's office. Imitating Abraham, he began keeping case histories of his classmates, jotting down anything odd or disgusting: how one boy pushed his pen nib underneath the skin on the back of his hand; how another kept picking a scab on his chin so the sore never healed; how one girl squeezed her eyes shut when she had to answer questions; and how another, the most beautiful in the room, drooled ever so slightly as she bent over her copybook in concentration. After making each entry, he stuffed the ledger under his mattress to hide it from his father.

Chapter 8

A week after school ended, Miriam Gottenberg arrived in Galilee. Miriam's mother, Emma—Abraham's sister-in-law—had died two months earlier, trampled by a runaway horse, Miriam had been told. Miriam's father, Hans, wrote Abraham the true story: Emma had just carried a tea tray into the sitting room of her employer, Mrs. Duncan Phelps, when Mr. Phelps pointed a gun at his wife and fired. Phelps, drunk, missed his wife and hit Emma. Hans's grief was confused by his satisfaction at having conclusive evidence for what he'd always believed: New York was a damned city. He decided to return to Europe. Emma's family ran a successful dressmaker's shop in Vienna and had offered Hans a job. In the same letter that described the tragedy, Hans asked Abraham to take in Miriam for a year. Once Hans was settled, he would send for his daughter.

Abraham had doubts about the arrangement. Having no daughters, he exaggerated the difficulty of taking care of a girl who was changing into a woman. Miriam was sixteen, Jacob's age.

Rosa wanted her to come.

"She's your niece," she told Abraham, "and she needs family."

Rosa regretted not having a daughter. She looked forward to Miriam's confiding in her.

"I want someone around I can share secrets with, the way you share secrets with the boys," Rosa told Abraham.

"I don't have any secrets with the boys," Abraham said.

"Not that I mind," she said. "It's natural. I'm sure I wouldn't be able to understand even if you let me in on them."

"What are you talking about?" he asked.

"It's how boys learn to live in a man's world," she said. "What would I want to know that for? I certainly don't care about hunting or fishing . . ."

"I don't hunt or fish," he said.

". . . Although, having lived with you for so long, I probably know a good deal about medicine," she said. "In fact, if I were a man, I think I'd be a good doctor. Sometimes I wish I were younger, so I could study medicine."

"Rosa," Abraham asked, "is something bothering you?"

"Bothering me?" Rosa asked. "Why no. I just think it might be pleasant to have a girl around the house."

They were sitting on the front porch, after the boys had gone upstairs. When Abraham shifted his weight, his wicker chair crackled.

A young voice spoke out of the dark of their front lawn: "Doc, my baby brother's sick. Pa says to come."

Abraham sighed and stood.

"You wait for me," he told the boy. "I'll get my things."

To Rosa he said, "I'll write Hans and tell him to send his daughter along."

Upstairs, Jacob and Hermann, playing checkers in Jacob's bedroom, overheard their parents' conversation.

"We'll have to take care of her all summer," Jacob said.

"You can," Hermann said.

The afternoon Miriam's train came in, Jacob and Hermann waited on the second-floor porch, watching the road to the railroad station.

Rosa hurried from the guest room, where she had made sure the pitcher was filled with warm wash water, to the kitchen, where she checked the ham baking in the oven, and back to the guest room, where she plumped the pillow.

"Don't gawk," she told the boys. "You'll make her feel unwelcome."

"She is unwelcome," Hermann said.

"I hope she would not be as unkind if something happened to your father and me—God save us—and Hans had to take you boys in," Rosa said.

"I'd like to go to Europe," Jacob said.

"I'd stay here," Hermann said.

"Here they come," Jacob said.

By the time Jacob, Hermann, and Rosa reached the back door, Abraham had dropped Miriam in the yard and driven the buggy into the stable. Miriam, in a gray cloak with a peaked hood, was squatting holding a dog's head with both hands and letting the animal lick her face.

"What's its name?" she asked before introducing herself.

"I don't know," Jacob said.

Hermann explained, "It's not our dog."

Miriam wiped her face. She didn't like dogs. Assuming this one belonged to the Gottenbergs, she'd let it lick her only to be ingratiating.

Miriam was pretty. Her hair was the red-yellow of a sparrow hawk's tail, and when it was not tied with a ribbon (as she usually wore it), it hung halfway down her back. Her eyes were pale blue, and she was watchful. Jacob once caught her scrutinizing his father. She glanced down guiltily when she heard Jacob enter the room. It was that guilty glance, not the attentive gaze, that disturbed Jacob.

What was she thinking that made her look away like that? Jacob wondered.

Her nose was narrow. Her nostrils, which seemed paper-thin, flared when she was interested or distressed. Her hands and her mouth were her only unlovely features. Her hands were narrow like squirrel paws, and her mouth was too wide. It looked like a clown's exaggerated grin when she smiled, but she rarely smiled. Most of the time she pouted in what she meant to be a skeptical frown, but which looked like an invitation to a kiss. All her life people had cooed over her. She didn't enjoy being treated like a doll, so she affected a hard manner. People assumed, correctly, that this toughness protected something tender. As a result, her toughness seemed one more charm. This often saved her from retribution when she was sharp, even nasty, but it also frustrated her. She felt no one took her seriously. No one, that is, except Hermann, who didn't see her toughness as an outward manifestation of an inner gentleness. He saw her toughness as toughness, her nastiness as nastiness. When she was sharp to him, he was sharp back. Because he made no allowances for her, she felt he was the only one who understood her.

"Want to see my *Yellow Kids?*" she asked Hermann a few days after she arrived.

Miriam saved the comics from the *New York World.* She loved the cartoon slum, which seemed modeled on the real slum in which she'd lived in New York, except the real slum had none of the liveliness that made the cartoon slum a circus. She loved the clothes that, drying on the lines, looked as cheerful as flags; loved the mongrel dogs that were more realistic than the goofy children; loved especially the cheerful urchin in the voluminous yellow nightgown, the Yellow Kid, who dominated the busy alley scene and who reminded her of a boy in the apartment next door. Although at least twice as old as the cartoon character, this boy had the same shaved head and slack smile. He'd been born "simple," her mother once explained. His family did not like having him around, so they kept him outside their apartment in the hallway, where, dressed in a dirty nightshirt, he stood for hours staring through a cracked window at the alley. He drooled and soiled himself, but he was friendly. When someone carrying something passed, he would gently put his hands on the parcel and walk along as though he were helping with the load.

"Why was he born simple?" she once asked.

"God punished his parents," her mother said.

Miriam wasn't satisfied with this explanation. The simpleton aroused her curiosity more than her pity. His behavior seemed to her not simple but complex. Everything he did was a ritual, from the way he placed his hands—thumbs always touching—on whatever anyone was carrying to the care with which he positioned himself next to the hallway window, always standing with his heels aligned to a crack on the floor.

Miriam's parents, more educated and with more social pretensions than most of their neighbors, tried to protect Miriam from a world in which they thought she—and they—did not belong. They forbade her to associate with the other children, who they claimed lived vicious lives, so Miriam, at first just for the sake of company and later out of a feeling of shared exile, spent hours with the simpleton. She tried to get him to talk. He blinked at her as though she were a stranger.

She found in the cartoon Yellow Kid the friendliness

she missed in the simpleton. Week by week, the cartoons took on greater and greater importance for her. She clipped them from the newspapers and hid them. Each colorful picture seemed a window in a wall of words, an opening into a world in which brutality was transformed into innocence. Miriam was amazed that someone could see joy in such a joyless scene.

In offering to share the cartoons with Hermann, she was being uncharacteristically amiable. Never before had she even told anyone she collected them. Hermann, who was lying across his bed working on his ledger, said, "I'm busy."

"What are you doing?" she asked.

Hermann sprang from the bed and slammed the door.

Miriam was convinced Hermann had been writing about her in a diary. That evening, while Hermann was doing chores with Jacob, Miriam sneaked into his room and searched for the ledger, which she found in the third place she looked: under his mattress. She smuggled it back to her room inside her blouse.

She locked her door, threw herself on her bed, and opened the book. She scanned a page quickly, turned to the next and the next, reading more and more slowly. The case histories of Hermann's friends fascinated Miriam. The observations were funny and heartbreaking. Miriam thought it was wonderful that Hermann could see his friends so clearly

Quickly leafing through the book, she searched for an entry on herself. There was a single sentence, under the date of her arrival. Hermann had written, "Today, after lunch, Pa picked up Cousin Miriam at the station."

Miriam rolled onto her back and stared at the ceiling. If she'd been keeping a diary, she'd have written a lot about Hermann. Not just because she liked him, but because he was somebody new, and new people were always interesting—at least in the beginning, when you were trying to figure them out. That was why she'd borrowed Hermann's ledger. She wasn't snooping. She was trying to figure him out.

She jumped up and found a pencil. She would return the ledger as soon as she made an addition. Out of respect as well as for revenge, she wrote a parody of Hermann's case histories, using Hermann himself as a subject.

That evening at dinner, Miriam could tell Hermann had read her work. He refused to meet her eyes. When anyone asked him anything, he answered in one or two words.

"Have you decided how you're going to spend the summer?" Abraham asked him.

Hermann muttered something.

"What?" Abraham asked, his fork and knife poised over his plate.

"No," Hermann said.

"I need some help in my office."

"No," Hermann said.

"You can start after breakfast tomorrow morning. First, go over the accounts. Then you can ride with me to Indian Orchard."

"No," Hermann said.

"Good. I'm glad that's settled."

Hermann looked at his father with a wild, despairing expression. It had been hard for him to rebel against Abraham, and he felt cheated out of Abraham's anger.

"I won't do it," Hermann said.

Abraham went on eating.

"I won't," Hermann said.

Abraham's lack of response was more terrible than the worst outburst could have been. Hermann scanned the table for something to break, something not too valuable.

Miriam followed Hermann's gaze. She didn't realize he wanted to smash something. She thought he was trying to save face by getting on with the meal.

"Can I pass you anything?" Miriam asked. She wanted to rescue him. "The salt? The pepper?"

In her eagerness to hand him the shakers, she knocked over his glass, spilling water into his lap.

Hermann threw himself sideways. His chair toppled. He sprawled against one of the table legs. Abraham, Rosa, and Jacob leaped to steady wobbling glasses, pitcher, candlesticks.

Hermann reared up on his knees, his chin just above table level, and screamed at Miriam, "Leave me alone!" To his family he said, "I don't want her here."

Miriam folded her hands in her lap.

"I hope you didn't hurt yourself," she said to Hermann.

After dinner, while Jacob was clearing the table, he noticed that Miriam's spoon had been bent out of shape and then straightened.

Jacob found her sitting on the front porch, darning a blouse. He held up the spoon.

"You're a stoic," he said.

She put her mending on the floor, took the spoon, and said, "It has to be washed."

At the door, she said in a low voice, "If you ever tell anyone . . ."

"You don't understand," Jacob said. "I admire you."

Miriam said to Jacob what Hermann had said to her: "Leave me alone."

Because Miriam wanted to fit into the family, she imitated Jacob and Hermann and started reading Abraham's psychology texts. At first Abraham was amused.

"When I see her struggling with one of those books," he told Rosa, "I want to put my arms around her and tell her she doesn't have to prove anything."

"Why do you think she's trying to prove something," Rosa said. "I don't think she's struggling. She asks good questions."

Miriam did ask good questions, and Abraham answered them. His answers grew longer and turned into anecdotes. All the old stories he used to tell his sons, stories they long ago had grown tired of, Abraham now told Miriam. She'd sit in his office while Abraham rambled on, finding new truths in the old stories. His index finger tapping the tip of his nose, he'd say, "Now here's what I want you to read for tomorrow."

Hermann, jealous of the attention his father was paying to Miriam, tormented her by demanding whatever book Abraham had given her. He'd leave the book in his bedroom unread. Jacob would sneak into the room, retrieve the book, and return it to Miriam, a favor she resented more and more.

"I can get it myself," she finally told Jacob.

But when Jacob did not get the books for Miriam, Miriam did not get them herself.

"Are you afraid of Hermann?" Jacob asked her.

"I don't want to cause trouble," she said.

"He's the one causing trouble," Jacob said.

"You're the one causing trouble," Miriam said.

As Jacob left the room, he knew she was studying him the same way she'd studied his father that time shortly after she'd arrived.

Miriam decided, that if Hermann couldn't find her, he couldn't demand her book. She began escaping into a field beyond the edge of town. In a grove of trees, the only one around for miles, she curled up in a hollow to read in peace. The trunks surrounding her were tall and straight, the bark fluted as Doric columns. Once, she fell asleep over her book and woke to find Jacob standing a few feet away.

"Why are you following me?" she asked.

"You shouldn't have to hide from Hermann," he said.

"Maybe I was hiding from you," she said.

"Do you want me to leave?" he asked.

She didn't answer.

Jacob sat against the trunk of a tree. When Miriam stretched out her legs, her skirt rode up over her calves.

"Do you want to kiss me?" she asked.

A speck of sunlight slowly moved up her cheek, stopped, and moved back down. Jacob knelt beside her. She closed her eyes and turned her face toward him. He kissed her. Her lips were chapped, covered with hard scales of dried skin.

"Put your arms around me," she said.

He did.

They kissed again—for a longer time. When they separated, Miriam said, "Leave me alone now."

"Why?"

"Because I want you to."

"Has Hermann ever kissed you?" he asked.

He expected her to get angry. Instead, she said, "If I tell you, I won't let you kiss me again. Do you still want to know?"

"No," Jacob said.

Miriam started reading. One page. Two pages. The beginning of the third.

Jacob interrupted her.

"Tell me," he said.

"Hermann never kissed me," she said.

After dinner that night, when the five of them were sitting in the parlor, Hermann asked Miriam if he could borrow her book.

"I'm almost finished with it," she said. "I'll give it to you when I'm through."

Hermann realized he shouldn't have asked in his parents' presence.

"I can wait," he said.

"Thank you," Miriam said.

She crossed the room and gave Hermann what seemed—to everyone but Jacob and her—an innocent kiss.

Chapter 9

That autumn, Abraham and Rosa took Jacob, Hermann, and Miriam to Omaha to the Trans-Mississippi Exposition.

Beyond the entrance rose spires, domes, colonnades, and crenelated towers. To Jacob, the architecture suggested the dwellings of genies and knights. It seemed as foreign as the Orient, as foreign as the past. To Hermann, it didn't seem foreign at all. It suggested the cities that would cover the country in the next century.

They lunched in a rooftop restaurant in the shade of a striped awning. There was no wind. The flags drooped. The sun blazed on the white stucco of the buildings. Below, the crowds dragged along the promenade, the women hidden by their parasols, the men in straw boaters. From the distant Plaza came the beat of the marine band's bass drum. Abraham let Jacob and Hermann each have a stein of beer. Jacob lounged in his chair, legs crossed at the ankles. The weight of the glass made him feel adult, in control of his destiny.

After lunch, they rode in a gondola. Miriam sat next to Jacob, who pressed his knee against hers. She changed position. He pressed his knee against hers again. Scowling, she moved away.

In the Horticulture Building, the air was moist and fragrant. Abraham reached into an exhibit and picked a scarlet anemone for Rosa, who hid the flower inside her coat. Miriam also plucked an anemone, one so purple it seemed black, and gave it to Hermann, who dropped it and walked on. Jacob picked up the flower and offered it to her.

"Keep it," she said.

In the Mines and Mining Building, Hermann asked Miriam, "Why don't you steal some of that gold for me?"

They'd rented wheelchairs and were being pushed through the hall by men in short white jackets and white caps.

"Please, slow down," Miriam told her attendant.

In his wheelchair, Hermann glided ahead.

Jacob rolled up beside her.

Miriam touched Jacob's shoulder.

"Can I have the flower?" she asked.

Jacob slipped the anemone out of his buttonhole. She threaded the stem through her hair.

For the next few hours, Miriam stayed at Jacob's side and ignored Hermann. At the Indian camp, she bought a blue bandanna, which she tied around Jacob's collar. He was both flattered by and ashamed of her attention, which was too maternal. He wanted to be tying a bandanna around her neck.

In the late afternoon, Abraham told Rosa, "Let's go back to the hotel and let the boys explore on their own."

"What if Miriam wants to explore on her own, too?" Rosa asked.

Abraham took off his hat and wiped his brow.

"If she were my daughter, I'd let her go," Rosa said. "And don't look at me that way."

When Abraham and Rosa left the fair, Abraham said, "Don't get into trouble."

Rosa said, "Have fun."

"This proves it," Jacob said. "Centaurs. The Minotaur. They all existed."

"It's a monkey sewn onto the tail of a fish," Hermann said.

"Where?" Miriam said. "The skin goes right down."

"What yokels!" Hermann said.

Miriam stalked off to the next exhibit in the sideshow. After glancing one last time at the withered brown corpse, Jacob followed. Hermann lagged behind, trying to find the line where the two halves of the creature had been sewn together.

There was a lady with a boa constrictor. The snake looked dead, and the woman had a cold. When the fakir got up from his bed of nails, you could see his back was covered with infected sores. The dog-faced boy, Hermann pointed out, did not have a dog face at all. The Smallest Man in the World stank of urine. The Tallest Man in the World had nicked his cheeks shaving.

Jacob accepted them all as wonders of nature. Miracles. Miriam agreed that they were wonders, but did not think they were miracles. She'd been reading in one of Abraham's texts about mutations. The poor people on exhibit were proof of life's inventiveness.

"'In nature, there are no monstrosities,'" Miriam quoted; "'there are merely experiments.'"

Hermann dismissed them all as what they were advertised to be: freaks. Within fifty years medicine would be able to prevent such deformities.

"That's what's miraculous," Hermann said.

"You have no imagination," Jacob said.

"You're the one without imagination," Hermann replied. "With your old-fashioned myths and legends. Mermaids and centaurs. There's nothing original in that. What takes real imagination is trying to figure out how to keep freaks from being born."

"What's imagination got to do with it?" Miriam asked.

"Let's go," Jacob said.

She balked. "I'm not ready," she said.

"She's your sweetheart," Hermann said to Jacob. "You can stay with her. I'm going to see the rest of the fair."

"Come on." Jacob grabbed her arm.

She slapped his face.

"All right," Jacob said.

He left the sideshow. Hermann and Miriam followed him into an arcade. Jacob plunged into the crowd. He didn't want to lose them, but he wanted them to think he was trying to.

At a bank of kinetoscopes, Jacob paused. Which machine should he try? Buffalo Bill's Wild West Show? A bicycle race? A parade of elephants? A minstrel show?

Hermann hunched over a machine which advertised the Fitzsimmons-Corbett fight. Miriam stood near him, but she was looking at Jacob, who ignored her and continued to stroll along the aisle. One of the kinetoscopes offered "The Dance That Drove Chicago Wild." Above the peephole was a picture of a hootchy-kootchy dancer. Jacob was embarrassed to look in that machine with Miriam watching, so he put his nickel in the next, which showed a temperance drama.

When Jacob left the arcade, Miriam tugged at Hermann's jacket the way the girl in the temperance drama had tugged at her father's coat. But Hermann, who was watching the Fitzsimmons-Corbett fight for the third time, ignored her. She ran after Jacob. Hermann took one last look through the peephole, slammed the side of the machine with his fist, and, before the film ended, hurried after her.

Jacob knew Miriam was following him and he turned their exploration of the fair into a game of follow-the-leader. They zigzagged through the Grand Court, around the statues that, livid in the lights from a nearby building, looked like corpses propped up on pedestals. Jacob wandered in and out of the portico of the Illinois Building, doubling back in such mazy loops that it became obvious to Miriam he was making fun of her. But still she followed—as Hermann, increasingly angry at Jacob's prank, followed her. If Jacob vanished, he had to be there to take Miriam home.

Finally, Jacob headed up to the relatively uncrowded Bluff Tract, the stretch of the fair lying along a high bank. The valley below was dark. Jacob had not realized how on edge the blaze of electric lights had made him.

Miriam gently took his arm. About a dozen feet away, Hermann's footsteps crunched on the gravel. Jacob shrugged off Miriam's hand.

"Jacob," she pleaded.

He became aware of a faint thudding, almost a feeling in his chest rather than a sound, like distant footsteps of a giant tramping through the dark, across the valley toward them. The noise was coming from a low building with a cluster of round chimneys, which was half hidden behind a viaduct. Jacob pushed open the door and entered.

The room was vaulted like a church, and high up on one wall, glowing like a stained-glass window at noon, was the open door of a furnace. Standing on a catwalk in the flare of the fire was a short man with shoulders so huge they looked like the humps of folded wings. On the opposite wall was his shadow, twenty times his size. He tapped the glass face of a dial as big as a clock and clanged the furnace door shut. Turning to face Jacob—and Miriam and Hermann, who also had entered—the man grasped the railing of his balcony, a minister about to preach a sermon; but although he was shouting at them, his voice was drowned out by the thudding of the generator, the noise Jacob had heard outside.

"He wants us to leave," Miriam yelled as she grabbed Jacob's arm.

Hermann grabbed Jacob's other arm. They started pulling him toward the door of the power plant. Jacob broke their hold and dashed over the tangle of pipes which covered the floor.

Miriam and Hermann tried to catch him, but he leaped the guardrail, clambered up the side of the generator, hoisted himself onto the drive shaft, and, straddling it, edged his way along until he reached the huge flywheel.

"He'll kill himself," screamed Miriam.

Hermann stood at the guardrail waving violently to Jacob. The worker on the catwalk was running back and forth, shouting.

Using large bolts for hand- and footholds, Jacob crawled down the flywheel, heading toward the floor—although by the time he reached the far rim, the turning of the wheel brought him not to the floor but to another catwalk halfway up the wall. Jacob dropped onto it, ran to a window, and climbed out.

He did not appear back at the hotel until midnight, hours after Miriam and Hermann had returned. He refused to say where he'd been. In bed, Abraham said to Rosa, "Why does he have to be so secretive?"

"Don't you have any secrets?" she asked.

"Do you?" he asked.

"Of course," she said.

She closed her eyes.

"Rosa?" Abraham said.

She already was breathing regularly.

"Rosa?" Abraham repeated.

Abraham was so absorbed in considering what his wife had said, he fell asleep wearing his glasses.

Miriam's father sent for her in November. He'd gotten settled in Vienna much faster than he'd expected. The night before she left she wept so hard she had to stuff the corner of her blanket into her mouth to keep anyone from hearing her. The whole family saw her off. As soon as they reached the depot, she hopped from the buggy and strode up the platform to the door of the waiting train. Abraham and Rosa followed with her suitcase and a basket of food. Jacob, hands in his pocket, slouched on the platform, hoping to catch her eye as the train pulled away. As soon as Hermann got the station hand to trundle away Miriam's trunk, he climbed back into the buggy.

On the way home, Jacob said, "You didn't say good-bye."

Hermann said, "Neither did she."

Chapter 10

The following autumn, in 1898, Jacob entered the University of Nebraska, where he yielded to the disreputable glamor of Jesse Singleton Parks, an ethnologist who as a young man had lived among the Pawnee Indians on the Loup River—and, according to student rumor, had ridden with the tribe's warriors to fight the Sioux and steal from whites. The most lurid story told how he and six Pawnee had raped a white woman near Kearney and then cut out her tongue to keep her from accusing him, a tale that had to be apocryphal since the only one who could have spread it was Parks himself, which he certainly would not have done. Parks, now sixty-two years old, had an old woman's face, a pinched spinsterish look: watery eyes, pursed mouth, skin so pale and smooth it seemed as though he never in his life had needed to shave. He was completely bald, the top of his head covered with brown spots. Class wits said he should have saved the scalps he'd taken.

Jacob used to wait for him outside the new library and walk with him the two miles to his house, a decrepit wood-frame building set nearly a hundred feet back on an over-grown lawn. The floorboards on the front porch were rotting. The latch was broken, so that even in winter the door, skewed on its hinges, was usually ajar, snow dusting the hall rug. At home, during the cold weather, Parks never took off his overcoat. Once, he missed a morning class. Because he always was punctual, Jacob was sure he'd died in his sleep. Running all the way to Parks's house, Jacob found his teacher upstairs in the bedroom, snoring, wrapped in his coat. One foot was tucked under a blanket bunched at the bottom of the bed. The other foot, uncovered, stuck straight up in the air. Through a hole in his filthy sock protruded his big toe, which, very pink and long, looked uncannily like a thumb.

His wife had died over a decade before, and Parks admitted to Jacob that he could not recall having cleaned the house since. Dishes encrusted with coagulated grease, dried egg, and rotting matter that could have been either animal or vegetable weighted down piles of papers and crowned stacks of books. While rummaging in a closet for a map Parks had drawn of Pawnee migration, Jacob found a coffee cup which had, curled up in its bottom, a dead mouse. When he showed it to Parks, the old man said it must have been his coffee that killed it.

Parks would reminisce for hours about his life among the Indians, and although he never mentioned any war parties, raids, or rapes, Jacob was rapt. He would dip his pen point and then, pen poised and ink drying on the nib, forget to take notes, forget even to light the lamps at sunset. Parks would fall silent, and Jacob suddenly would notice that it was night. All the by-now-familiar furniture, transformed in the dark, looked like large cardboard cutouts in an unlit museum diorama, the ottoman domed like an Indian lodge, the surviving frond of a dying palm plant feathered like a war bonnet, and the sofa, one side of its back higher than the other, humped like a bison. Jacob would gather his books and papers, whisper, "Good night, sir," and walk home to the room he rented near the college.

In warm weather, the streets would be crowded with people, strolling in twos and threes. As he passed each group, Jacob overheard fragments of conversation, disconnected phrases, which seemed like bits of torn-up book pages that had been scattered to the winds. Even the most banal was a seductive clue to the lives those strollers led. Jacob could understand how his father had been lured into his study of people's oddness. But he wanted to resist the temptation to become curious. He wanted to preserve the fragile mood conjured up in him by listening to Parks's stories. So he tried to close his ears to the world around him. He hurried hunched over, as though he were carrying a lit candle and trying to keep its flame from being snuffed out by the breeze.

Jacob preferred the walk home in cold weather. Fewer people were on the streets, and they all were rushing to get someplace warm. Jacob ambled along the shoveled sidewalks, shivering a little but not uncomfortable. Every so often, he slipped on a patch of ice and, to regain his balance, waved his arms like a minstrel dancer. Snow half erased the world. On the blank drifts, Jacob sketched imaginary Indian villages. He tracked dogs and cats, following the deep footprints across lawns and down alleys. He stalked men in top hats who were late for dinner. When the sky was clear, he would throw back his head, the cold slapping against his neck like an executioner's blade, and look for the evening star, the Pawnee goddess Atira.

His boardinghouse smelled of lavender, because his landlady hid sachets everywhere—balanced on the tops of picture frames, behind books, on windowsills, on top of the grandfather clock, dangling from the rope portiere . . . When he lit the gas jet in his room, the flame caught with a *whuup*, the sound of a willow switch being whipped through the air, and he always narrowed his eyes, remembering the half dozen times his father had thrashed him. Sitting in the rocking chair by his bed, he would try to study, but his attention invariably strayed. He was distracted by everything—even the familiar furnishings of his room. The multicolored quilt on his bed. ("Each patch came from a different dress of mine," his landlady had bragged, a disclosure that made Jacob feel uncomfortable every time he slid under it.) The bureau top, cluttered with a bone shoehorn, a handful of coins, a package of Duke's smoking tobacco, his shaving mug with its brush, the bristles as neat as a well-tended goatee, a clothes brush with an ivory handle, a few detachable cuffs still circled by their paper bands. His mirror, which reflected his own face, looking unfamiliar with its new black beard. He tried to imagine what it would be like to be sitting around a campfire in an Indian village, what it must have been like for Parks, who had gone to live with the Pawnee when he was Jacob's age. Jacob would toss his book onto his bed and, after considering and rejecting taking another walk, throw himself onto the bed next to the book and again try to study.

"Biology. Chemistry. Your grades are terrible," Abraham said when Jacob went home to Galilee for Easter in 1900. "How are you going to be a good doctor?"

They were sitting across from each other, knee to knee, in Abraham's consulting room. To keep from looking away, Jacob stared into his father's eyes with such intensity that he began to feel dizzy. The light in the room changed—outside, a cloud moved in front of the sun—and Abraham's pupils dilated. There was a red fleck, like a blood spot in a fertilized egg, in the white of his right eye. Staring so hard gave Jacob the feeling he was not looking at his father at all.

"I'm not going to be a doctor," Jacob said.

Abraham leaned forward so abruptly, Jacob at first thought his father was about to attack him. Instead, Abraham put one hand flat against his son's chest and crushed him against the back of his chair. With his other hand, he magically produced a gold watch. Almost simultaneously, Jacob realized three things: he had noticed, without having been aware of noticing, that his father was not wearing his watch chain across his vest, as he usually did; his father had held the watch concealed in his hand since the beginning of the discussion; and his father had intended to ceremoniously present the watch, a symbol of the tradition Abraham assumed Jacob would carry on.

"Take it," Abraham said.

"I can't," Jacob said.

"Take it!" Abraham shouted.

Jacob took it. He felt the warmth of his father's hand on the metal.

"What do you want to do?" Abraham yelled.

The question, shouted right in his face, was so startling that Jacob laughed.

Abraham reared, as if Jacob had slapped him.

"I'm going to study Indians," Jacob said, trying, by sounding exceptionally calm, to make his father's behavior seem outrageous.

"But I need you," his father said.

Jacob, still staring into his father's eyes, imagined that if he blew into his father's face the delicate rays of his father's irises would scatter like the white down of a dandelion seed ball. He would not have to suffer under his father's disapproving gaze.

"Why don't you say something?" his father yelled. "Indians! Jacob, why?"

Parks repeated the same question when Jacob returned to school and, seeking sympathy and advice, told him what had happened. They were sitting in the dark in Parks's house. Parks had just talked for two and a half hours, describing his last hunting trip with the Pawnee. An autumn hunting trip. They'd found very little game. For the first time since these sessions began, Jacob had trouble paying attention. Over and over, he debated with himself whether he should say something to his teacher. Although they were comfortable talking about Indians, they were uncomfortable talking about anything else. Jacob decided it probably was not proper to inflict his personal problems on Parks—which was why he did, as though going against his better judgment were a test he felt he had to pass.

"Why do you want to study Indians?" Parks asked.

Jacob was astonished. He did not know what to answer.

"I . . . How can you ask that?"

"Why shouldn't I ask that?" Parks asked.

"Because you study Indians," Jacob said.

"That doesn't mean you should," Parks said.

Parks rocked, the regular creak of the chair and thump of his feet on the floor filling the silence. At last, more quietly than before, he repeated, "Why do you want to study Indians?"

"For the same reasons you do," Jacob said, thinking that he had answered the question.

"I've forgotten why I do," Parks said.

Jacob was afraid to say anything. What could he say? Scold his teacher? For what? Trapping him? Or telling the truth? Jacob hoped Parks was not telling the truth. He was embarrassed for the old man. He did not want to hear any confession.

"I was a rebellious boy," Parks said, "as you are. My father wanted me to become a minister. He was a minister. My grandfather had been a minister. I didn't want to be a minister. When I went to live with the Pawnee, I did it as a lark. I don't know what I expected. I'm sure I didn't expect to stay very long. But I didn't go home for three years. By then I had . . ."

He paused. Jacob listened to the creak-thump, creak-thump of his rocking.

"I was," he continued, "like a man who jilts a girl he loves and hates and, to prove he doesn't care for her, marries another he's indifferent to."

"You don't like studying Indians?" Jacob asked.

"It's not a matter of like or dislike," Parks said. "I haven't been unhappy doing it."

Another pause. He added, "It's what I've done."

Walking home that night, Jacob tried to answer for himself the question his father and teacher had asked, a task as difficult as trying to recall a forgotten name. A number of times he was sure that if he just could focus his attention better he'd be able to articulate what he felt; but he couldn't concentrate.

"I know what I want," he muttered.

His mind wandered from thinking about studying Indians to remembering how magical it was to sit in his attic corner reading fairy tales, legends, and mythology. And he realized that when he imagined the scenes of Indian life Parks described, the mental pictures were as bold and as vividly colored as the Howard Pyle illustrations in his childhood copy of *The Merry Adventures of Robin Hood.*

That summer, Jacob laid siege to a small band of Omaha Indians who lived on a reservation on the banks of the Black River, seventy miles from Galilee. The camp was small: a dozen dome-shaped lodges; a horse pulling up clumps of grass with a sideways jerk of its head; a wagon missing one wheel, which lay not too far away, perhaps where it had rolled to when it had come off, its rim broken and most of the spokes snapped. As Jacob drove his buggy along the narrow track, no more than a footpath that had been worn in the grass, he passed a dog dragging a bundle on a frame made of two parallel poles lashed to some cross braces. The Indian who walked beside the dog, a young man in baggy trousers and a checked shirt so faded it at first seemed to be a solid pale color, did not look at Jacob. In the camp, two infants in ragged gray shirts which ended at their swollen bellies were sifting dirt through their fingers and laughing. When they saw Jacob, they stopped playing and stood. Both were so emaciated that the normal hiplessness and dwarfish legs of babies were exaggerated. The boy's genitals, especially the taut purple scrotum, looked sore. They dashed out of sight around one of the lodges, upsetting a wooden bowl of red corn seeds, which lay spilled in the dirt like bloody teeth.

Jacob had chosen to study the Omaha Indians because they were nearby, but he felt the choice was appropriate since their name meant "Those who go against the current"—which was what he felt he was doing.

A man with the profile of an ancient Caesar ducked out through the doorway of the nearest lodge. He wore an old United States Army coat, which was missing most of its buttons. He crossed his arms while Jacob climbed down from his buggy and approached.

"Welcome to our village," he said in good English. "I am Ernest F. Boone."

Jacob explained who he was and where he was from.

They shook hands. Boone's face was webbed with a network of fine lines, as though it had been shattered. Around his neck he wore a thin gold chain partially hidden in a fold of skin.

"I am looking for Chief Black Dog," Jacob said.

"I am Chief Black Dog," Boone said.

The Indian's hair was shoulder-length. The slight breeze blowing it out to one side made it look alive.

Jacob told Boone that he wanted to stay with them and learn their ways.

"Many people come and ask that now," Boone said. "I say no."

Jacob tried to sway Boone, but his arguments sounded false to himself. They must have sounded dishonest to Boone. He was trying to answer the same question his father and Parks had asked him—why did he want to study Indians?—and he could not. Boone kept smiling, but refused to change his mind.

"You think I am unfriendly?" Boone asked at last.

Jacob nodded, expecting Boone to continue, to deny the charge or beg Jacob's understanding, but the Indian said nothing more. He simply gazed into Jacob's face. Jacob realized with shock that Boone was using on him the same tactic he'd used two months before on his father: staring intently in order to avoid looking away and appearing weak. Jacob climbed into his buggy and drove off.

The next day, about mid-morning, Jacob crossed the river downstream and drove through a field of five- and six-foot-high sunflowers that thumped against the wooden sides of his buggy. He stopped opposite the Omaha camp. He made a big production of unhitching his horse, putting it out to graze, cutting a thin branch from a tree, trimming and sharpening it, and sitting on the bank facing Boone's lodge. Methodically, he cleared a space in front of him, grabbing handfuls of grass, yanking them up by the roots, the clumps dangling as he held them high, like scalps. He tamped the dirt so it made a smooth firm surface and, using his sharpened stick, started drawing meaningless hieroglyphs with as much concentration as he could muster. He knew that if he wanted to attract curiosity he had to do something active. The trap was set and baited.

The day was hot. Under his shirt and coat, sweat trickled along Jacob's sides and down his back. His neck was chafed where his stiff collar rubbed. Heat bugs made their high-pitched metallic whine, which after a while sounded to Jacob as if it were not the noise of an insect but a ringing in his ears.

After three hours, a young man—Jacob thought it was the Indian he'd seen the day before walking with the dog—wandered to the edge of the opposite bank and casually tried to see what Jacob was doing, but the distance from bank to bank across the river was too great and the angle was wrong. Still, he stood watching Jacob.

For two more hours, the Indian hardly moved at all and Jacob continued writing with the stick, tamping the dirt, and writing some more. His mouth was so dry the insides of his cheeks stuck to the sides of his tongue, which felt swollen to twice its normal size. His eyes were so dry that every time he blinked it felt as though he had paper cuts across his corneas. But he was afraid that if he interrupted his meaningless activity he would lose his audience. So he continued writing, tamping, writing.

Shortly before sunset, before he left for the day, Jacob felt an electric shock rack his body. The moment after, he had the odd sensation of floating somewhere in the air above and behind his body, looking down at himself, still scrawling in the dirt with a stick, and at the Indian on the opposite bank, still watching, as motionless as a statue and obviously, it seemed to Jacob, trying to prove that he had more stamina than Jacob did. In the instant before his floating consciousness was slammed back into his body, Jacob, wondering about the two figures below—himself and the Indian—thought, "Why are they doing such silly things? How odd."

The next day, the Indian was waiting when Jacob drove to the bank opposite the Omaha camp. Jacob sat down where he'd sat the day before; but, unlike the day before, he took off his coat, collar, and cuffs, and he kept within arm's reach a water-filled tin canteen he'd borrowed in town. About two o'clock in the afternoon, three boys sauntered out from behind a lodge and settled on the opposite bank on either side of the first Indian. Jacob put down his stick with a deliberate motion, as though it were part of a ritual. He took a swallow of warm water from the canteen. Again with a deliberate motion, he picked up his stick, drew in the tamped dirt, and, without glancing at the Indians, began to talk in a voice loud enough to carry across the river.

He introduced himself, described the room in which he lived in Lincoln and the house in which he'd grown up in Galilee, and told them about his father, mother, and brother. He described the first time he'd gone to the circus, where he'd marveled at the parade of elephants, the Petrol-cycle, which was a sort of motorized wheelchair, and the ostrich, which, when he held out a biscuit for it, swallowed his arm up to the elbow—or so he remembered. He described the Colt Army pistol he owned, his mother's stereoscope with its slides of Biblical scenes, and the soda fountain at Lorenz's drugstore; its vaselike cut-glass straw dispenser, its shiny spigots with their black nozzles and the black balls on their handles, and its marble counter, mottled like headcheese. For five hours Jacob droned, stopping only to take sips of water, which he tried to make look ritualistic. By sunset he was hoarse and desperate for things to say, croaking on about the smell of the icebox on a hot day, the jar of bust cream he once found hidden in his mother's bureau, and the copper teakettle that, when water boiled, whistled through a bluebird on its spout.

On the third day, a dozen Indians, old and young, male and female, were assembled on the bank across the river, waiting for Jacob—who, before sitting down, stripped off not only his coat, collar, and cuffs, but also his shirt. He rolled up his trousers and pushed his long-john sleeves over his elbows and his long-john legs over his knees. Along with the canteen of water he'd brought two packages of slippery elm lozenges. With as much solemnity as if he were performing a religious ceremony, he placed a lozenge on his tongue and drank some water. Then he began his pitch.

He'd stayed awake most of the night before, making lists of what he could talk about, so although he was exhausted and not looking forward to the day's ordeal, he was well prepared. He sang "A Bird in a Gilded Cage," "When You and I Were Young, Maggie," "Little Annie Rooney," and "Grandfather's Clock," which for some reason was a hit. When he bellowed, with all the appropriate histrionic gestures, "But it stopped—short—never to go again—When the old man died," everyone on the opposite bank grinned and nodded with such unanimity that they looked like a windup toy.

He discussed the United States' new Open Door policy toward China; recited Robert Browning's "The Pied Piper of Hamelin"; debated with himself the advisability of Bryan's recent nomination for the Presidency; imitated how his father rocked at mealtime; mocked the prissy way his brother dressed, as though Hermann felt his clean clothes were going to dirty him, and mimicked the unpleasant expression—the wrinkled nose of someone who smells something foul—Hermann habitually wore while reading; told a joke about trolley cars; and, as twilight fell, described how when he was twelve he once had a dawn rendezvous with a girl on whom he had a crush. She appeared at her back door in her nightgown. They crouched under her parents' arbor, the winy reek of the ripe grapes heavy in the air around them, and watched the sun rise.

That night, Jacob again stayed up, planning his monologue; but when he arrived opposite the Omaha camp the next morning, only one man, Boone, was waiting for him. They sat down on either side of the river and smiled at each other.

"You've been telling stories," Boone said.

"I'm running out," Jacob said.

"White men don't run out of anything," Boone said, "especially words."

"I do," Jacob said. "At least, out of words that make sense."

Boone sighed.

"What have you been writing in the dirt?" he asked.

"Nothing," Jacob said.

Boone covered his mouth with a hand. Jacob wondered if that was Boone's first real, not just polite, smile.

"You're unfair," Boone said. "You've forced me to do something I don't want to do. Because you have told us your stories, I must tell you ours. I am no less generous than you."

For one and a half days, the same length of time Jacob had talked, Boone described for Jacob the life of their village. When he was through, he said, "Now you go home."

On his way back to Galilee that night, Jacob whipped his horse. As he racketed across the prairie, he shouted to the sky the sacred song of the Omaha: "Na-kon'da. Here needy he stands; I am he."

Although he continued his Indian studies with Parks, Jacob dutifully followed his father's advice and for the next year worked hard at biology and chemistry. In the spring, he came home to Galilee to—as he'd written to Abraham—"have a serious talk."

"Come into my office," Abraham said.

Jacob had arrived the night before, and he and his father were having coffee in the kitchen. Rosa, her back to them, stood washing the breakfast dishes. Whenever she passed the table on her way to the stove to get a fresh kettle of hot water, she avoided looking their way.

"I'd rather walk in the yard," Jacob told his father. "When I'm in your office I feel like a little boy."

It was early. There was still dew on the grass. The toes of their shoes got wet and turned dark.

"I've decided to go to medical school," Jacob said.

Abraham stopped.

Jacob walked on a few paces, still staring at his feet, before he faced his father. Instead of looking pleased, even joyful, as Jacob had expected, Abraham looked furious. His forehead and cheeks were red. His lower jaw was pushed out, and his lower lip was stretched back, exposing his teeth, so he looked like a pickerel.

Jacob was hurt and confused.

"Why are you so angry?" he asked. "I'm doing what you want."

"You're not doing what *you* want," Abraham said. "You've got no conviction, no character."

Jacob hugged his father. Abraham stiffened; but when Jacob did not let go, he tentatively embraced his son.

"I do need you," Abraham said. Tapping Jacob's shoulder, indicating surrender the way Hermann used to when Jacob pinned him in one of their wrestling matches, Abraham said, "I've got to get back to work."

Chapter 11

Unlike Jacob, Hermann, who entered the University of Nebraska in the autumn of 1901, intended from the start to be a doctor. Also unlike Jacob, who was interested only in ideas, Hermann was interested only in facts. He filled his mind as though he were packing a trunk, making sure every corner was used, no space was wasted. In the afternoon, after the last lecture of the day, he locked himself in his rented room to read and take notes in a handwriting so tiny and precise it looked foreign. At first he ate his meals in his boardinghouse with the other students who roomed there, all of whom Hermann disliked. Food made some of them boisterous. They joked, told stories in loud voices, and grinned as they chewed, exposing their teeth, glistening with saliva. Others withdrew as they ate, their faces slack as they cut their meat in what struck Hermann as haphazard, illogical ways. One student, a farm boy with flaring nostrils and three lateral creases across the bridge of his nose, especially infuriated Hermann with his method of carving. Instead of slicing a bit off the end, he cut his portion in half, cut the halves in half, cut the quarters in half, and so on until his plate was filled with tiny pieces of meat. Hermann was horrified and fascinated. He could not stop watching—partly because he enjoyed the rush of outrage which watching released in him. He also was gratified by the dependability of the hog-nosed student's bad manners. In a world that seemed increasingly random, Hermann could count on getting angry at meals. But by the end of two weeks, habit had diluted his anger. To keep from losing his rage, Hermann expressed it.

"Stop that!" Hermann yelled, standing and throwing his crumpled napkin into his plate. A corner landed in a pool of gravy. As the cloth absorbed it, a stain moved up the napkin in a swelling arc—which seemed to mirror a swelling Hermann felt in himself, a lightness as though he were filling with joy, the thrill of doing something irreversible. To make the thrill more intense, he yelled, "You're disgusting! All of you!"

The hog-nosed student guffawed and, trying to keep from spitting out the food in his mouth, stretched his chin forward and clapped a hand over his dribbling lips. One by one, the others at the table started to laugh. Hermann fled.

From then on he ate in a nearby restaurant, which had a white-and-black-checked tile floor. He always sat at the table farthest from the door, his hat and coat hung where he could keep his eye on them, and he always ordered the same dishes, jotting down each item and its price in the pocket diary he carried. After the waiter left, Hermann put his pocket watch on the table, where with its spring top opened it looked like an oyster that had spilled off a plate. He gave himself half an hour to eat.

He always ate alone, turning down all dinner invitations —especially from Jacob, whom he tried to avoid. One overcast evening, when Hermann was hurrying home from the restaurant, he spotted Jacob across the street, standing in the middle of a circle of young men, all of whom seemed to Hermann preposterously attentive. Jacob was gesticulating as he talked. His hair, which he'd let grow so long he looked like a performer in a Wild West show, whipped back and forth, got in his eyes (impatiently, he brushed it away) and his mouth (he shook his head and spit out the strands). None of that seemed to bother Jacob's friends.

Hermann tugged his hat down over his face and quickened his already quick pace. Behind him, he heard his brother call, "Wait."

Hermann did not stop.

Jacob whistled.

Hermann walked even faster. He nearly ran.

Jacob was running.

A block from Hermann's boardinghouse, Jacob caught up with his brother and fell into step beside him.

"Hey," Jacob said, out of breath. Above his beard his cheeks were rosy, and his eyes glittered from the exertion of the run. He looked healthy and happy.

"I guess you didn't hear me," Jacob said, offering Hermann an excuse for his evasive behavior.

Hermann didn't slow down.

"Who are you trying to protect?" Hermann said. "Me or you?"

"The family," Jacob said.

"Pa and Ma aren't here," Hermann said, "so you don't have to pretend I'm happy to see you."

"But I'm happy to see you," Jacob said.

Hermann stopped. So did Jacob.

"Do you want me to pretend?" Hermann asked.

"I think you are pretending," Jacob said.

"You think I really am happy to see you?" Hermann asked.

"I don't think you hate me," Jacob said.

He rubbed his cold hands together, cupped them over his nose and mouth, blew into them, and rubbed them together again.

"You should wear gloves," Hermann said.

"Why didn't you stop when I called you?" Jacob asked. "Are you all right?"

"Yes," Hermann said.

"Classes—" Jacob started.

"Fine," interrupted Hermann.

"What do you do in your spare time?" Jacob asked.

"I have no spare time," Hermann said.

"Where do you hang out?"

"I don't hang out."

"Where do you meet your friends?"

"I have no friends."

"You sound proud of that," Jacob said.

"I am."

"Why?"

"Leave me alone," Hermann said.

Jacob cupped his hands over his face again. Through them, he said, "Cold nose."

"I can't talk to you when you look so ridiculous," Hermann said.

"That's it," Jacob said. He circled his brother, an Indian around a wagon train. "You're ashamed of me," he said.

Slowly, with Jacob still circling him, Hermann edged forward.

"You're not a serious person," Hermann said.

Jacob stopped circling Hermann, who continued edging up the street.

"I don't know if I can make you proud of me," Jacob said, his voice getting louder as the distance between them got greater. "But I'm going to make you like me. You used to!"

By now he was shouting.

"You're wrong!" Hermann yelled as he turned up the boardinghouse walk. "I never did!"

The following day, Jacob showed up at Hermann's room. He was carrying a vase of frosted blue glass, which Hermann took at the door as though Jacob were handing him a gun. He didn't invite Jacob in.

"Very expensive," Jacob said. "I'm going to have to go without dinner tonight."

"Go without beer," Hermann said. "Here."

He shoved the vase at Jacob, who, refusing to take it back, raised his hands over his head, as though Hermann were sticking him up.

"I thought maybe you'd take me out to dinner," Jacob said, "so I won't go hungry."

"Sell the vase," Hermann said. He kept shoving the vase at Jacob. "I don't need it."

"You will," Jacob said, his hands still over his head. "I'm going to bring you flowers next time."

"Take it!" Hermann shouted.

"No," Jacob said.

Hermann slammed the door. Jacob dropped his hands. Hermann opened the door. Jacob raised his hands again.

"Look," Hermann said. "I'm going to let it fall. If you don't catch it, it'll smash and you'll lose your investment."

"The vase isn't what I was investing in," Jacob said.

"I'm going to do it."

"Go ahead."

The muscles in Hermann's cheek worked. Hermann found it hard to deliberately break anything of value.

"I'm going to," he said, although now he did not sound threatening. He was pleading with Jacob to stop him.

"Go ahead," Jacob repeated.

Hermann dropped the vase—which thudded and rolled on the floor, but did not shatter.

Jacob started to smile.

Hermann, also starting to smile, tried to force the corners of his mouth down, which made him smile even harder, until he was fighting to suppress a laugh.

"Well," Jacob said. He thought their conflict could not survive the ridiculous. "Shall we go to dinner?"

Hermann, still trying to keep from laughing, kicked the vase out of his room and slammed the door in Jacob's face.

The next day, Jacob waited for Hermann outside the boardinghouse and followed him to the restaurant. Jacob sat at Hermann's table. Hermann tried to ignore him.

"I know a better place to eat," Jacob said.

"I'm used to this place," Hermann said. "And I'm used to eating alone."

"Why do you want to be so boring?" Jacob asked.

"If you don't like the company, leave," Hermann said.

"Have you ever heard me give the Omaha mourning chant?" Jacob asked.

"Don't embarrass me," Hermann said.

"Then let's go," Jacob said.

The waiter started toward them. Hermann waved him away.

"Good," Jacob said. "Tonight you'll start a new life."

Shrugging on his overcoat, a new raglan that smelled like wet fur, Hermann said, "I like my old life."

Martinelli's Saloon was jammed. Smoke stung Hermann's eyes. The noise—clinking glasses, laughter, shouted orders—made him wince. The smells—cat piss, stale beer, and vomit—sickened him. Two fans slowly revolved, one of them rattling. The metal ceiling, stamped with a repeating pattern of laurel crowns, was black with soot from the potbellied stove in the middle of the room. Built into the wall behind the bar were mahogany columns, which supported a pediment decorated with bas-relief satyrs' faces like a theater's proscenium arch.

As Jacob passed, he was greeted with grins, grunts, and nods. He acknowledged them with an all-encompassing wave.

"You're popular," Hermann said.

Jacob blushed. He was still young enough to be embarrassed by the affection he evoked in others.

"You must waste a lot of time in here," Hermann said.

Jacob's blush deepened, this time from anger. He realized Hermann's comment on his popularity had been not praise but criticism. As he saw Hermann slyly smile at the effect of his words, Jacob also realized that Hermann had intended him to mistake the criticism for praise.

They stopped at one of the tables. Five young men lounging over beer welcomed them with various gestures—raised hands, raised eyebrows, raised steins—and salutations—"What do you say?" and "Hey, Jake!"

"Jake?" Hermann asked. At home, his brother always insisted on being called by his full name, Jacob.

"I want you to meet some of my friends," Jacob told Hermann.

"Can't we go somewhere quieter?" Hermann said.

"If it were quieter," Jacob said, "it wouldn't be any fun."

"It's not fun," Hermann said.

The men around the table wore their hats indoors. Jacob left his on. Hermann removed his.

Jacob introduced his brother around. People jerked Hermann's hand up and down, throwing him off balance. He slipped on some beer and grabbed Jacob around the shoulders to catch himself. Misunderstanding the hug, thinking it fraternal, Jacob affectionately patted Hermann's arm—which Hermann angrily withdrew. People's mouths moved, but in the hubbub Hermann couldn't catch their words, so he nodded and scowled and rubbed his eyes, which burned so much he could hardly keep them open.

Jacob beamed at everyone around the table. "They like you," he said.

"I'm hungry," Hermann said. He slipped his watch from his vest pocket and snapped it open.

"Put that away," Jacob said. "You're not on any schedule tonight." He tried to stuff the watch back into Hermann's pocket.

"Careful," Hermann said, "I had to buy this myself. Pa didn't give me one, like he did you."

Jacob stared at his brother in amazement. Hermann blushed.

"Do you want mine?" Jacob asked. "I'll trade."

Hermann pretended not to hear.

"I've got to get back to work," he said, standing.

"What?" Jacob said, also pretending not to hear and standing.

Hermann folded some dollar bills into Jacob's hand. "Enjoy your dinner," he said.

Jacob grabbed the sleeve of Hermann's overcoat with one hand. With the other, he waved the dollars at the waiter.

"For everyone at the table," Jacob called.

"I don't want to buy drinks for them," Hermann said.

"They like you," Jacob repeated.

"I don't care," Hermann said.

He pushed through the crowd toward the front of the bar, but Jacob, still hanging on to his sleeve, acted as a rudder and steered Hermann to another table.

"Sit," he said.

Hermann sat.

In this corner of the room, it was not as noisy. The piano man had stopped playing. And the air seemed less smoky—or Hermann was getting used to the smoke. At the other half of the table, three students were playing a silent game of poker. To ask for cards, they held up fingers; to call, they nodded. Everything was done quickly and with no argument, as though it were not a game but a ritual or a mime performance.

"Can we get something to eat?" Hermann asked.

"Beer first," Jacob said.

"I don't want beer," Hermann said. "I want to eat and go home."

"Why don't you enjoy yourself?"

"I do enjoy myself."

"How?"

"Many ways."

"Yes?" Jacob said.

"Look," Hermann said. "I'll have one beer and then go."

"Remember how we used to wrestle for dessert?" Jacob asked. "Let's wrestle to see who pays for the beers."

For the first time since Jacob had sat down across from Hermann in the restaurant and threatened to give the Omaha mourning chant, Hermann relaxed. He leaned back in his chair and crossed his arms.

"Here?" he asked.

"Out back," Jacob said. "You want to, don't you?"

"No," Hermann said. He got up and left.

In the dark street, the air was cold. From a few blocks away came the clopping of a horse and the rattle of a wagon. Hermann buttoned his coat and pulled on his gloves. It would snow before morning.

Hermann had gone only half a block when Jacob jumped him. They tumbled to the ground and rolled in the street.

"Stop it!" Hermann said. "You're getting me dirty!"

Jacob, who was trying to get a headlock on Hermann, didn't answer. Hermann ducked. Getting his knee between their bodies, he pried Jacob off. Panting, they faced each other on hands and knees. The wind rolled Hermann's hat down the street in and out of the street lamps' light. It was a new hat.

Hermann lunged at Jacob. They grabbed each other

around the chest. Each tried to force the other down. Just as Hermann felt his hold slipping, Jacob, as he used to when they were boys, gave up. He crumpled under Hermann. Looking up with laughing eyes, Jacob said, "You win. I pay. Let's go inside, get the beers."

"You son of a bitch," Hermann said.

He stood. Tugging his coat first one way and then the other, he twisted around trying to see the damage.

"I'll pay for the cleaning," Jacob said.

Hermann, now checking his pants legs, didn't answer.

"I'm sorry," Jacob said.

Hermann wandered off, stopping every few feet to examine something or other: his coat elbows, the seat of his pants—or as much as he could see of it by pulling his pants around and craning his neck. He found his hat in the gutter and brushed it on his sleeve. By the time he felt respectably put together, Jacob was nowhere in sight. Hermann almost wished Jacob had come after him. He would fight him. If Jacob let him win, he would make sure he never tried that trick again. Hermann imagined cracking Jacob's head on the pavement—and then closed his eyes against the thought. He realized he'd been walking down the middle of the street like a drunk.

He decided to take a shortcut home. In an alley, from behind the door of what looked like a livery stable, he heard people yelling, "Kill him! Kill the bastard!"

Hermann pushed the door open. Dozens of untrimmed kerosene lanterns flared and smoked, casting more shadow than light. Nearly a hundred men, a few well dressed, but most poor laborers, farmers who'd lost their farms, and young men who'd abandoned families to see the world and had gotten only as far as Lincoln, pressed toward a ring which had been jerry-rigged in the center of the room. Inside that slack rope circle, two men fought. One of them—the larger—had a fuzz of blond hair and a scarred face. He wore red shorts over black tights.

The other fighter, shorter and broader than the first, had a huge chest that seemed inflated, as though he lived out of his element and like a man under water was holding his breath. He wore street clothes except for his shirt and jacket, which he'd stripped off, revealing the pathetically threadbare top of his long johns. He waved his fists back and forth in front of his face like a baby in a cradle as the other man regularly smacked him with punches so solid they sounded like claps.

Hermann used to enjoy reading about boxers, and had been fascinated by the kinetoscope version of the Fitzsimmons-Corbett match he'd seen at the Trans-Mississippi Exposition, but he'd never seen a live boxing match.

This match was passionless and mechanical—and therefore terrible. The tall fighter hit the other man with the awful disinterest of a carpenter driving nails. And no matter how much punishment the short fighter took, he refused to fall.

With each blow, Hermann winced.

"Why doesn't he get out?" he asked.

"Fifty dollars prize money if you last three rounds," said a man on Hermann's right.

He wore a bowler and carried a cane. His face was fat and glistened with sweat. His mustache was waxed and crimped up—impudently, thought Hermann—at the ends. He craned his neck so he wouldn't miss anything.

"Brute," Hermann muttered.

"Nah," said the man in the bowler, who thought Hermann was referring to the tall fighter. "He's just trying to make a buck. Like the other guy. Say, wouldn't you let some guy beat you up for fifty bucks?"

"I wouldn't," Hermann said.

"I guess not," said the other, glancing at Hermann. "You and me, we don't need the dough. But how about this? You're down on your luck; what can you do? I say the law against fights is a shame. A game like this, it's almost charity."

"And you're doing your Christian duty watching it?" Hermann asked.

"Don't misunderstand me," the other began. Something in Hermann's tone stopped him. He looked Hermann up and down again, more slowly. "Hey," he said, "I'm no mug. Don't go high-and-mighty on me. I work in a bank."

At first Hermann pretended he was staying because it was a good opportunity to study an interesting case—or, more accurately, interesting cases, since he was surrounded by men who watched the fight in states of high excitement, their eyes glittering, their mouths open—like starving men waiting for their dinner. Then, with the shock of someone waking from a doze in public, he realized that for the past few minutes he'd been taking no notes on the audience. He'd been mesmerized by the boxers. The short man fell to his knees and sagged sideways to the floor. Hermann was standing on tiptoe to see. All around Hermann, men were booing the winner.

The champion strode around the ring, chest out, head back, hands on hips and elbows to the sides. He looked comical, as though he were doing an imitation of a rooster. Hermann felt sorry for him. In his moment of triumph, he was hated by so many.

Hermann worked his way to ringside, which was easier to do than he had thought. People assumed he was one of the gamblers who were circulating, trying to be unobtrusive as they collected their winnings and paid off their debts.

The fighter's manager called in a hoarse voice for other volunteers, but no one stepped forward. For five minutes he harangued the crowd without success. The fighter, now slumped on a three-legged stool in a corner of the ring, looked embarrassed. Hermann felt a fresh undertow of sympathy for him.

"I'll do it," he said.

Up to the moment he'd spoken, he had not even considered fighting. As he ducked under the rope, he wondered if this was the first time since he was a boy that he'd done something without weighing the pros and cons.

Hermann took off his winter gloves, hat, coat, jacket, tie, and shirt. He worked methodically and carefully folded each item before putting it on the floor outside the ring. The crowd loved his fastidiousness and cheered this dandy who dared take a beating. His opponent was annoyed.

"Tell him to hurry up," he croaked.

The manager ignored his complaint. Instead, he said, "Listen to you. You keep smoking cigars and drinking that rotten whiskey and some kid like this"—he jabbed his thumb at Hermann—"is going to lay you out."

Some kid like this.

For a moment, Hermann saw himself through their eyes: ridiculous. No, worse than ridiculous—a nonentity, one more rube to be battered.

How many men has he knocked down? Hermann wondered.

As the manager laced a pair of gloves on Hermann, he said, "You know the rules. No biting. No kneeing in the groin. No wrestling."

In the lenses of the manager's glasses Hermann saw himself reflected grotesquely, his forehead and chin impossibly narrowed and his nose swollen so it took up most of his face.

Hermann was not afraid of pain. Jacob was strong. In the fights with him Hermann often had been hurt. But he dreaded having to box with one eye on the clock, having to last three rounds. That, he thought, would be as hard as lying in bed with insomnia: enduring the sheer unpleasantness of the wait.

To his surprise, the match passed so quickly he felt

cheated. Afterward, he went over and over the few moments he could recall.

They had faced each other in the center of the ring and circled so slowly, so hypnotically, that the room, not they themselves, seemed to revolve. The boxer kept squinting and wrinkling his nose, the way Hermann had seen squeamish students do in a dissecting class. His forehead was ringed with beads of sweat, each as large and round as a rivet, as though the top of his skull were bolted on.

When the boxer started punching, Hermann almost laughed. It seemed such a ridiculous thing to be doing. The blows did not hurt. He also seemed to be moving so leisurely that Hermann had plenty of time to anticipate him—although for some reason Hermann could not make his body respond fast enough to take advantage of his anticipation. The more the boxer hit Hermann, the more Hermann felt dissociated from the fight. At one point—in either the second or the last round—Hermann had a clear impression that he and the boxer were engaged in a common enterprise, although what the job specifically was eluded him: something to do with hoisting a heavy load or winding up some complicated piece of machinery. Each punch seemed to turn a ratchet another notch.

Then they were no longer fighting. Hermann felt abandoned—like an infant left alone by its parents. He looked around for the boxer. He almost loved him. He wanted to throw his arms around him, affectionately butt heads. But the manager kept getting in his way, muttering, "That's enough. That's enough."

When Hermann looked out at the audience, one face after another abruptly came into focus: grinning faces. Everyone was cheering, waving their hats.

"He did it!" they were shouting.

To Hermann, they all seemed puny, pitiful. The only person in the room who deserved his esteem, the only one with whom he shared any common feeling, any bond, was his opponent.

Hermann turned away from the audience—languidly, he thought, almost regally. But with mounting disgust he realized that instead of walking with dignified precision he was staggering, drooling. He jerked his head up so he would not look pathetic. The light, which had seemed dim, suddenly flared so brightly that Hermann had to squint—as the boxer had done at the beginning of the fight.

Was he hurt before we started? Hermann wondered. From other matches earlier in the evening? Where is he?

Hermann brushed aside the manager, who was thrusting the prize money at him, and gazed at his opponent. The boxer was standing, as dazed as Hermann, his face bloody.

Hermann could not remember throwing even one punch.

The boxer's name was Billy London. As a boy in Hadley, Massachusetts, he'd been the town bully—although when he beat up his schoolmates he never thought he was being cruel. He thought he was being funny. When he was sixteen, he ran away to Boston, where he fought for a living. For the first time, he met men who were stronger than he was, and it seemed natural that they should knock him down. He never held a grudge against another fighter, even when the other man fought dirty. He too fought dirty when he could get away with it. He was not ambitious. He once beat Jake Kilrain, and could have gone on to become a challenger, but training was too much trouble. He was content to travel the country and fight in small towns, losing once in a while, mostly winning.

He never brooded over a fight after it was over. He

hardly remembered it. So when Hermann came back two days later, London did not think of their second bout as a return match. The fastidious way his opponent folded his jacket and shirt was familiar, but he assumed—to the extent that he considered it, and he hardly considered it at all—that this was another, equally fastidious Nebraskan. For all he knew, the whole state was filled with men who cared about their clothes.

Hermann found London's indifference galling. For forty-eight hours, ever since he'd staggered into the cold night, happy at lasting three rounds, he'd thought of nothing but boxing again with London. Over his books, he brooded about the fight. During lectures, he smelled the stink of London's breath. At night, he dreamed of the cool, Olympian contempt he'd felt for the audience. His obsession disturbed him. He vowed to think no more about boxing—only to find himself sneaking around a corner in his mind as though he could indulge in a fantasy without letting himself know about it. At last, he went back to the livery stable.

When he met London in the center of the ring, Hermann said, "I'm going to win this time."

London shrugged. The stronger man would win; the weaker man would lose. It had nothing to do with them personally—although this fastidious young man, like so many others, appeared to take it personally.

London's manager was warming up the crowd, shouting about "this champion of the plains who once again will match skill and cunning with the Boston Behemoth."

London yawned. This was his last night fighting in Lincoln. He would sleep for a day. Then he and his manager would head back East—although even the prospect of going home to Massachusetts elicited only a lizardlike pleasure. He had a vague memory of the taste of oyster stew, which did not ascend into his consciousness so much as rise, a bilious bubble, into his throat. He belched and spit.

Hermann, who thought London was spitting to express contempt, also spit. Seeing a frown lengthen London's face, he thought he'd made London angry.

But London's frown, like a newborn's smile, betrayed little about his mood. When Hermann spit, London surfaced just long enough to check out the disturbance, his glance as lazy as a crocodile's. Then he sank back into himself. His frown was only the trace of his strenuous effort to pay attention to his surroundings.

London fought like an actor who knew his lines so well he could walk through his part. Hermann fought like an actor who had never been given a script, usually blundering but occasionally improvising with brilliance. He noticed that from time to time London took a deep breath, squared his shoulders, and slightly dropped his guard, a lazy habit from years of boxing amateurs. Dozens of times it had gotten him into trouble, but London fatalistically figured that if his opponent was good enough to take advantage of the lapse he deserved to win. It was easier to accept some losses than to break the habit. Halfway through the second round, when London took a deep breath and squared his shoulders, Hermann slugged him in the belly, once, twice, three times, four times, five times, inexpertly but effectively alternating fists, working away like a solemn child pretending to be a choo-choo train. With each blow, London made a little hop backward until he crashed through the rope, sat down hard outside the ring, and, his legs stretched out in a V in front of him, leaned forward and vomited the rich dinner he'd eaten earlier that evening.

The manager tried to drag Hermann back across the ring, but Hermann knelt beside London. He held the boxer's shoulders until the retching stopped.

"You all right?" Hermann asked.

London, whose head seemed rigidly fixed to his neck, swung his whole upper body to glare at Hermann. He was enraged not because Hermann had knocked him down but because he'd shown kindness.

"We'll," London gasped, "fight again."

London took out a quarter-page advertisement in the newspaper, challenging Dapper Dan—which was what, in his weak attempt at wit, he called Hermann—to a third fight. Because of the laws against boxing, the wording was not explicit, but everyone understood what was meant. And everyone wondered who Dapper Dan was, whether he would accept London's challenge.

"London will massacre Dan," Jacob said.

"You're sure?" Hermann asked.

"I bet fifty dollars on it."

"Where did you get the money?"

"I pawned my watch."

"Pa's watch!" Hermann said.

"After the fight I'll get it back," Jacob said.

"And if London loses?" Hermann asked.

"He won't," Jacob said. "Why are you smiling?"

On leaving his brother, Hermann went to the Palmer House, where London and his manager were staying. In an alcove, surrounded by cushions the oxblood color of boxing gloves, Hermann agreed to fight on the condition that they do it privately, no audience.

"I don't want to be recognized," he said.

"We can't do it without an audience," the manager said. "We won't make any money."

"I'm not doing this one for money," London said.

Dressed in a suit and tie, London looked shrunken, tired. The skin at the corners of his eyes and mouth was yellow, as though once he had been plated with gold and the pummeling he'd taken through the years had rubbed the metal off everywhere but there.

"You're passing up a great chance," the manager said.

"I'm getting the chance I want," London said.

"So am I," Hermann said, thinking of Jacob's bet.

The next night, they met in the livery stable, just the three of them. Without the crowd the building seemed huge. The rafters soared upward, vanishing into the dark. The manager lit lanterns and put them on the ground around the ring. As Hermann and London circled each other, the shadows of the ropes crisscrossed them.

The first time London hit him, Hermann felt as though his cheek had been splashed with hot wax. Blood dripped onto his arm. London was wearing not padded but skin-tight gloves with heavy stitching along the knuckles. Every punch he landed ripped open Hermann's flesh. By the end of the first round Hermann's face was cut so badly pieces of skin hung in tatters. He looked like a corpse that had begun to putrefy.

Early in the second round, London smashed Hermann's nose. The injury didn't hurt, but every time Hermann tried to breathe he inhaled blood. After the round ended, the manager tried to stop the fight. Both Hermann and London ignored him.

In the third round, London worked on Hermann's eyes. By the end of the fight Hermann's left eye was swollen closed and his right eye was barely open. To see through it, Hermann had to tip his head back and to the side. He sat on the ground as the manager unlaced his gloves. Hermann struggled to hold on to a thought long enough to grasp it. *Jacob would get back the watch.*

"The mirror," London said.

The manager produced a mirror.

"Let him see," London said.

The manager held the mirror up to Hermann's face. Hermann tipped his head back and to the side. He looked monstrous. He started to make an awful wheezing, choking noise.

"He's crying," the manager said.

London grinned.

"Let's go," he said.

They blew out the lanterns and left. Hermann, alone in the pitch-black building, sat on the ground. The manager was wrong. He wasn't crying. He was laughing.

Before he left town, London announced his victory in another newspaper advertisement. Jacob redeemed his watch and with his winnings bought Hermann a new hat to replace the one damaged in their scuffle. When he went to Hermann's boardinghouse to deliver it, Hermann refused to open his door. Jacob hung the hat on the doorknob and sauntered down the hall whistling. Hermann waited until he heard Jacob descend the stairs before he opened the door and snatched the hat. Although he was in his nightshirt and dressing gown, he plopped the hat on his head.

Hermann told his landlady he was sick. She brought him meals on trays, which she left outside his room. He didn't want anyone to see his battered face. For the month and a half it took him to heal, he didn't go out—not even to exams. The school suspended him.

Hermann arranged to go back to Galilee and help Abraham. Jacob accompanied him to the railroad station. They walked slowly, their shoulders occasionally touching.

"I always thought I was the black sheep," Jacob said. "Now I can't even get thrown out of school. It'll look like I'm copying you."

"You resent that?" Hermann asked.

"I don't want to be the good boy," Jacob said.

"I don't want to be the bad boy," Hermann said. "We're both stuck."

They walked in silence.

"You're going home to help Dad," Jacob said. "That's good. I'll never do that. When I get out of school, I'm going . . ."

"Where?" Hermann asked.

"New York," Jacob said, "Alaska."

"I don't believe it," Hermann said.

"Do you want to bet?" Jacob asked.

Hermann laughed.

"What's so funny?" Jacob asked.

"You and your bets," Hermann said. "All right. If I win, I get your watch."

"And if I win?" Jacob asked.

"You keep it," Hermann said.

"That's not much of a bet," Jacob said.

Hermann said nothing.

"I accept," Jacob said.

They shook hands.

"We won't know who wins for years," Jacob said. "What if we forget?"

"I won't forget," Hermann said.

MIRIAM: 1915–16

Chapter 12

One autumn afternoon in 1915, six years after Abraham returned from Worcester to make his middle-of-the-night announcement to his sons, Jacob was straddling a branch of an apple tree, smoking his pipe and watching a workman repair a rain gutter on the old Stutz farmhouse, now the Main House of the Gottenberg Clinic. The tree was his retreat. Often, he perched for hours, brooding about patients. In the branches around him hung odds and ends he'd nailed up: ribbons, an Indian mask of a tutelary spirit with an eagle's beak and terrible eyes, glass that dangled from strings and flashed in the sunlight, a silk hat, and a tobacco tin, which the rain had scrubbed shiny.

A woman pedaling a bicycle turned from the Galilee Road onto the dirt path which looped through the clinic's grounds. She wore a gray knickerbocker suit. With its ballooning legs and sleeves, it made her look like an Oriental dancing girl. Around her waist was a blue sash. On her head was a straw hat, tied across the crown and under her chin with a scarf. The costume, although long out of fashion in the East, was novel, even brash, in the Black River Valley.

She stopped below Jacob, swung off her bicycle, and propped it against the tree trunk. She untied her scarf, took off her hat, and shook her head.

She just missed being beautiful, Jacob thought. Her face was too long, her mouth too wide, her lips too thin and her eyelids too heavy.

She clapped the hat back on her head and tied the scarf loosely around her neck. With a quick knee bend, she smoothed the knickerbockers over her buttocks.

"Did you bicycle all the way from town?" he asked.

Below him, the woman looked left and right.

Jacob laughed. His pipe, clenched between his teeth, spouted ashes, which rained down on her as she looked up.

"Sorry," he said.

She pulled a handkerchief from her sleeve and dabbed at her face.

"What's all that?" She waved at the trinkets in the branches. Although she had a German accent, she spoke English fluently.

"My totem and talismans," he said.

"Why are you in the tree?" she asked.

"Among the Araucanians of Chile," Jacob said, "the *machi*—that is, the sorceress—is initiated by climbing a nine-foot tree, her ascent into the heavens. She returns to earth with the gift of healing."

"You're the sorceress?" she asked.

"The Araucanians also practice ritual sex change," he said.

"Why would any man want to become a woman?" she asked.

"Are you a suffragette?" he asked.

"I'm a doctor," she said. "Miriam Gottenberg."

"Miriam?" Jacob said. He spoke her name wonderingly.

"Are you a patient here?" she asked.

"Sometimes I think I am," Jacob said. "I climbed up here to escape the crazy doctors who run this place."

"Why don't you come inside with me?" she said.

Jacob wondered if she recognized him, if she was only going along with his pretense in order to make him seem as childish as he probably was being. But how could she recognize him? They had not seen each other for over a decade and a half. She certainly had changed—for the worse, Jacob thought. Enough, anyway, so he hadn't recognized her. And he had the added disguise of the huge beard he'd been growing since college.

"Have you signed on?" he asked.

"Signed on?" she repeated.

"Are you here to work?"

"We can talk about that on our way inside," she said.

Since she thought he was a patient, she had no intention of continuing a real conversation with him. His joke was not turning out the way he'd expected, but he didn't know how to end it without leaving Miriam with the impression that he'd been trying to make a fool of her.

"Good apples," he said.

He plucked one and tossed it to her. She flinched but caught it.

"Don't be afraid to take a bite," he said. "I'd think you'd be delighted to get thrown out of this paradise." He waved at the flat fields surrounding the clinic. From his perch he could see the neighboring farm, where cattle grazed, their white faces looking like skulls.

"Where would you rather be?" Miriam asked.

Jacob rubbed his back against the tree trunk like a bear.

"Something strikes you as amusing?" Miriam said.

"I like my father's surprises," Jacob said.

"Your father?" she asked.

"Abraham Gottenberg."

"Is he your doctor?"

"You really think I am a patient?" he said. "I'm Jacob." When her expression didn't change, he said, "Jacob Gottenberg."

"I see," she said.

"Miriam," he said, "I'm not a patient confusing himself with his doctor. I really am Jacob. Your cousin."

Her expression still didn't change, but it seemed to Jacob she was fighting—what? Jacob wondered. A smile? A frown?

"It's not proper for a doctor to be up a tree," she said at last. "If I were your patient, I wouldn't trust you."

"If you were my patient," Jacob said, "I'd try to find out why you're so worried about what's proper."

Grabbing her bicycle, she headed down the path.

"Welcome to Galilee," Jacob called.

She spun around and threw the apple at him.

A little after five o'clock that evening, Hermann hurried out the front door of the Director's House, the most recently completed building on the clinic grounds. It was a yellow-painted Queen Anne mansion with a tower room, which served as Abraham's study, a high-pitched slate roof, which in the late afternoon sun flashed like a signal mirror, and a wide porch, which swept around the entire house, giving it a nautical air. Hermann disapproved of its ornate style. It reminded him of Captain Nemo's submarine in *Twenty Thousand Leagues Under the Sea.* He, Abraham, and Rosa had moved in during the first week in September. Jacob stayed in the old house in Galilee and rode the two and a half miles to the clinic on a smoke-colored horse he called—to Hermann's annoyance—Trauma.

"You trivialize everything," Hermann complained.

When Jacob began riding bareback, Hermann begged Abraham to intervene, but Abraham said what he always did when his sons quarreled: "Work it out between yourselves."

One morning, fortified with a cup of black coffee and a cigar, Hermann entrenched himself in a wicker chair on the front porch of the Director's House. He'd armored himself in his best clothes for this confrontation, even though it meant choosing style over comfort. His dress overcoat was thin. After half an hour in the sharp wind, he draped a blanket around his shoulders.

When Jacob rode up, Hermann hailed him.

"I want to talk to you," he said.

In his buffalo fur coat, Jacob looked like a shaggy beast crouched on the horse's back.

"I can't talk to you like that," Hermann said. "Come here."

Ducking his head, Jacob guided Trauma up the steps and onto the porch.

"You're crazy," Hermann said.

"Is that a professional or fraternal opinion?" Jacob asked.

The horse nuzzled Hermann's cheek.

"Get that off!" Hermann shouted.

Jacob backed Trauma down the steps.

"You're making the clinic look bad," Hermann said, "riding around like a damn Indian."

Jacob pointed at the blanket around Hermann's shoulders. "You look like an Indian, too," he said.

A few days later, as Hermann was crossing the clinic grounds, Jacob trotted past with Trauma decked out in bows, bells, tiny winking mirrors, and paper flowers. On the horse's head was an ivy garland.

"Stop it!" Hermann screamed.

He ran up to the horse and ripped off the decorations. Trauma reared, tossing Jacob, and galloped to the other side of the field.

Jacob limped to Hermann. Both clenched their fists.

"If you hit me . . ." Hermann said.

Suddenly, Jacob bent down, grabbed the ivy garland, which had fallen when the horse reared, and plunked it on Hermann's head.

That night, Hermann forbade Jacob to use the stable behind the Director's House. So Jacob kept Trauma in the stable behind the Staff House, another new building, a few hundred feet down the Galilee Road at the far end of the clinic grounds. To offset the bad impression made by Jacob's riding to work like a savage, Hermann bought a Packard touring car. But in that farm country an automobile, particularly such an elegant one, was odder than a horse ridden bareback, even one rigged out in bells and paper flowers.

The day the car was delivered, Hermann chugged into Galilee. Jacob, eager to see the machine, was headed in the opposite direction, from his house in town to the clinic. They met at Indian Creek, Hermann on one bank, Jacob on the other. The bridge was so narrow only one of them could cross. Hermann floored the accelerator. Jacob galloped. A woman and her three children stopped walking along the roadside to watch. Just as Hermann's front wheels reached the bridge, Jacob swerved and leaped the creek. The woman and children cheered Jacob. Hermann ignored them. Eventually, the town would catch up with him; with every passing year Jacob's Indian-style riding would seem more and more strange.

Hermann paused on the front porch of the Director's House. The lawn was still littered with scraps of lumber. He slipped a pen and notebook from his coat pocket and jotted a memorandum to Bobby Dombro, the clinic's handyman. For five weeks he'd been trying to get Bobby to clean up the mess. But Bobby was one of Jacob's worshippers, which meant he ignored Hermann. Hermann jotted a second memorandum, a note about Bobby's dereliction, for the file he was collecting to show his father. He wanted to convince Abraham to choose a successor. As long as both brothers held equal power, the clinic would continue to be run inefficiently.

Hermann put away pen and notebook and took out the watch he'd won years before when Jacob had returned to Galilee.

Seven minutes late.

In the Main House, Hermann peeked into the dining room to make sure everything was ready for dinner. On the two long tables, silverware gleamed. Every glass reflected the fire which blazed in the fireplace. But the tablecloth was not even. It hung more over one side than the other. Hermann slipped out his pen and notebook and jotted a memorandum.

As he went down the narrow hall beside the staircase, he smelled boiled beef and cabbage. Without being aware of it, he licked his lips. But out came pen and notebook again. This was the second time in a week they'd had boiled beef and cabbage. His memorandum to the cook told her not to repeat herself so often.

At the end of the hall were two coat trees, one on either side of the door to the solarium. Hermann counted coats. Except for the staff on duty and Abraham, everyone was here, even Jacob. His buffalo fur was not hung neatly from one of the scrolled arms but tossed over the top, enveloping all the other coats. Hermann heaved it off, almost toppling the tree. Cursing Jacob, he hung the fur coat properly.

Abraham had started the tradition of gathering the professional staff in the solarium at five o'clock every evening except Sunday. Now, however, he rarely came, and Jacob was erratic in his attendance, so Hermann usually held court. Sitting in a wing chair in the middle of the room, anointed by the warm rays of the setting sun, he felt like the crown prince of a great colonizing power. Doctors, nurses, and attendants, each with a different professional orientation—satraps of the provinces of Electrotherapy, Hypnotism, Nutrition, Massage, Zinc Phosphate, Oxide of Iron, Belladonna, Cold Baths, Sleep, Sexual Abstinence —deferred to him, reported to him.

But this evening, when Hermann entered, Jacob, wearing a necklace of pale blue Egyptian tomb beads, sat in the wing chair, surrounded by half a dozen members of the staff, who turned toward Hermann, their faces momentarily blank.

"Quite a surprise," Hermann said to Jacob. "You don't usually grace us with your presence."

"I'm just the appetizer," Jacob said. "The main course'll be here in a minute."

Jacob was too casual. The surprise to come would be great. Hermann hated surprises. They always seemed to be ambushes.

When Abraham and Miriam entered, Jacob watched his brother's face.

Abraham's beard billowed down his chest like smoke. He waited until everyone was silent. As though continuing a speech he'd begun on another occasion, he said, "I have the highest confidence in every one of you. Otherwise, you wouldn't be working here."

He always makes a compliment sound like a threat, Jacob thought. He enjoyed Abraham's theatricality, but since he shared the trait, he didn't take it seriously. Often, he made fun of his father, mimicking Abraham's oratorical pose, feet spread, one hand on his hip, the other waving in the air as though he were doing a Balkan peasant dance. Hermann thought he was being insolent. He really was being affectionate, struggling to humanize Abraham to counteract the tendency Hermann and most of the staff had of idolizing him.

Abraham boomed about his goal of having the most comprehensive psychiatric care in the country, the need to take on as wide a variety of therapeutic styles as possible—a speech Jacob had heard many times before.

Abraham's tone changed. The set speech was replaced by Miriam's credentials: studied at the University of Vienna, attended Freud's lectures, wrote a useful thesis on the psychology of fashion. Abraham launched into anecdotes Miriam had let slip in her nervous reunion with him. She was mortified. The longer he spoke, the higher she held her chin. After lectures—Abraham said—Miriam used to stalk Freud through the streets of Vienna, pumping up the courage to accost him. Merrily, Abraham waved his hand over his head in great circles as though he were about to leap into a Highland fling. He beamed at Miriam, who was paralyzed with shame.

Jacob winced in sympathy with her. He knew his father's inadvertently gorgon stare. If Medusa had been like Abraham, she had looked at mortals with nothing in her heart but love and been puzzled when they turned into stone.

Combing his beard with his fingers and staring at the ceiling, Abraham rambled on about Miriam's psychoanalysis with Wilhelm Stekel and about how before the war broke out she'd left Austria for England, where for the past few months she had been trying to establish a psychoanalytic society—"unsuccessfully, I might add," Abraham said.

Everyone in the room laughed except Jacob and Hermann.

After Abraham's speech, Jacob went to her.

"I'm sorry I teased you this afternoon," he said.

"Jacob," she said, "I'm not the sixteen-year-old girl you used to play with."

Hermann stationed himself near the library table, waiting for Jacob to stop monopolizing Miriam. He was startled by the affection he'd felt when she was introduced—more than startled, frightened, as if this slow flooding of love threatened to undermine the very foundation of the life he'd built ever since, seventeen years before, she'd climbed on the train without glancing back.

Across the room, Jacob kept touching her on the shoulder, hand, arm, shoulder again, like a spider attaching threads first to one spot, then to another as it secures its prey.

Hermann interrupted a colleague who was droning on about a patient and excused himself.

At Hermann's approach, Miriam turned away from Jacob. She and Hermann shook hands, both leaning back slightly.

"Do you remember the exposition in Omaha?" Hermann asked.

"Of course," she said.

Jacob, annoyed at Hermann's interruption, said, "I remember a lot more than that."

"Jacob," she said, "you're still so competitive."

The dinner bell rang.

"Stekel often quotes a Greek writer," she told Jacob. " 'If a strange woman crosses my land I must impregnate her, a strange boy must offer me his anus, a strange man must yield me some other form of pleasure.' " Satisfied that she had shocked him, Miriam entered the dining room.

"Formidable," said Hermann.

Jacob said, "I think I'm in love."

Chapter 13

The next morning, when Miriam entered the Main House foyer, she heard music coming through the closed double doors of the library. Its bouncing melody, naive as a child's hopscotch chant, kept getting interrupted by a slide trombone. She never before had heard anything like it, and she hated it; but since she was more curious about things she disliked than things she liked, she slid open the doors.

Inside, Jacob was dancing with a tall woman in a loose gown. She was lovely, but her beauty was not so much the presence of attractive features as the absence of unattractive ones. Her face was as simple as a doll's; and, like a doll, she looked worn rather than aged. Her blond hair was cut so short she was nearly bald. Instead of making her grotesque, this made her look majestic, the priestess of an ancient religion.

A round oak table stood in a corner of the room. On it were a gramophone with a brass horn and half a dozen leather-covered albums. The music ended. Jacob put on another record and cranked the machine. The woman squatted and clawed at her head, trying to grab enough hair to pull. Her face went slack, as though the bones within had crumbled.

The new song was a Viennese waltz played on what could have been a merry-go-round calliope, the melody going up and down like painted horses as the *oom-pa-pah*s got louder and softer. Jacob took the woman's hands and raised her. In his arms, she calmed, her face again becoming lovely, her manner stately.

But when the tempo of the song speeded up, she spun away from him, whirling around the room faster and faster.

"Stop her," Miriam said.

Jacob noticed Miriam for the first time. "Get out," he said.

"For God's sake," Miriam said, "turn off the music."

"Get out," Jacob repeated.

Turning to go, Miriam bumped into Hermann. Standing in the doorway next to Hermann was a giant, over six and a half feet tall, with a chest as broad as a tombstone. His name was Rudolph Kriger. He was the attendant who helped with violent patients.

"That's all, Jacob," Hermann said.

When he went to lift the needle from the record, Jacob grabbed his wrist. They grappled silently, ignored by the spinning woman.

Miriam looked up at Kriger, who she suddenly realized was no more than a boy, twenty-one years old at the most.

The spinning woman staggered. Jacob released Hermann's wrist and whipped around to catch her. Hermann grabbed the record and cracked it across his raised knee.

Jacob knelt on the floor, the woman cradled in his arms.

"You have no right," he told Hermann. "She's my patient."

"Not anymore," Hermann said. "She's Miriam's."

"Mine?" Miriam asked.

"I told you before breakfast," Hermann said to Jacob. "It's the Director's decision."

Except in intimate family gatherings, Hermann called his father the Director.

"Not until Pa tells me himself," Jacob said. To Miriam, he added, "Put on another record."

"Please, Jacob," Hermann said. "Don't." He pointed at the woman in Jacob's arms. "Look at her."

She was squeezing her eyes shut, a child trying not to hear her parents quarreling.

"Oh, Maggie," Jacob said.

He helped her up. Gently, Kriger led her away. As she passed Miriam, Maggie pressed his fingertips to Miriam's lips. Miriam took her hand. Under Maggie's fingernails was blood from clawing her head.

Once she was gone, Jacob asked Hermann, "Couldn't you wait until after the session?"

"Your sessions make her worse," Hermann said.

"Better," Jacob said.

"Screaming at night is better?"

"Better than never making any sound at all."

"She's not even supposed to be out of her room," Hermann said.

"Where she digs at her hair unless we straitjacket her," Jacob said. "Didn't you see her? She was dancing."

"Like a top," Hermann said. "You just set her spinning. Jacob, you don't know the harm you're doing."

"You drag her off," Jacob said, "don't even give me a chance to—"

"Your own fault," Hermann interrupted. "You can't get away with ignoring orders."

"Orders!" Jacob said.

"Do you think I'm lying?" Hermann asked.

"No," Jacob said. "But why didn't Pa tell me?"

After Hermann left, Jacob cranked the gramophone and put on another record, "I'd Rather Two-Step than Waltz, Bill."

"Does this happen often?" Miriam asked.

"Never before in front of a patient," Jacob said.

He slouched around the room, straightening a picture here, adjusting a throw pillow there. When he got to the window, he shouldered aside the maroon drape and pressed his forehead against the cold glass.

Outside, trees leaned in the wind. Hermann, clutching his overcoat closed at the neck, worked his way up the path toward the Director's House.

Without turning, Jacob said, "When I got out of medical school I wanted to go to the Yukon, somewhere up north, live with a tribe we hadn't touched yet. But Hermann was off at medical school. Pa needed me. So I came back. I was only going to stay until Hermann graduated. But when he got home, I stayed on. There never were enough doctors in the valley. Then Pa decided to start the clinic, and he asked us if we'd go East, specialize, make contacts. I was ready to climb on the first train out of Galilee. It took a year before we left. Pa sent Hermann to New York to learn psychoanalysis from Brill and me to Boston to study neurology with Putnam. Hermann wanted to go to Boston, and I desperately wanted to go to New York—and not just for Brill. I used to read about the Tenderloin the way some kids read about sailing down the Mississippi. Romance. If I couldn't study the savages in the Yukon, I wanted to study the savages in New York. Still, when I left for Boston I felt like Marco Polo, off to the Orient to bring back spices. I stayed two years. Just before I left, I was offered a job there. I asked for a week to think it over. The day before I had to decide, I went to a circus. After the show, I talked with one of the acrobats. I asked him what circus life was like. He told me a story.

" 'There was a manager of a circus who had a pet dog,' he said. 'And the circus was doing a lot of one-day stands. Every night the dog would bury a bone outside the manager's wagon; then it would go inside. While the dog slept, the circus would pack up, move to another town, and set up. Now, a circus always sets up in exactly the same way, so it always looks the same no matter where it is. Anyway, in the morning the dog would trot out of the wagon and go to dig up its bone. No bone. It would sniff around, puzzled, and finally give up. That night, it would get a new bone, which it would bury again in the same place outside the wagon. It would go inside the wagon to sleep, the circus would move, and the next morning, no bone. The dog lived a long time. Every night of its life, it buried a bone. Every morning, it dug where the bone should have been and found an empty hole.' "

Jacob faced Miriam.

"I turned down the job," he said. "I didn't want to dig empty holes all my life."

"You could have made a new home there," Miriam said, "like I'm doing here."

"I'm not you," he said.

The music ended. Jacob put on another record.

"Anyway," he said, "if I left, my brother would take over the clinic, and I don't like my brother's methods."

"Are they so terrible?" she asked.

"Not terrible," he said. "Just by the book. He wants to run the clinic like an army. He forgets to—"

"Treat patients like individuals?" she interrupted, smug at having anticipated Jacob's thought.

"No," he said, "love them."

"You sound like Stekel," she said. "He always quotes Paracelsus: 'The only thing we doctors can give our patients is love.' "

"Another quote," Jacob said. "Last night, about sex. Today, about love. Which is your motto?"

"It depends," she said, "on whether I'm defending territory or being a host. As a doctor, my motto is the second. In a clinic, a patient is a guest, not an intruder."

"And not as a doctor?" he asked.

"That also depends," she said.

She waited for him to ask, "On what?" But he didn't.

"At least, as a doctor," he said, "you're on my side."

"I'm not taking sides," she said.

Jacob quoted back to her, " 'The only thing we doctors can give our patients is love.' "

"But you can't love them all," she said. "So to help them, most of the time you have to go by the book. Like Hermann."

Jacob picked up the pieces of the record Hermann had broken. He fitted them together on the table.

"I hear Hermann is very good," Miriam said.

"In his way," Jacob said, "he is."

"I hear you are, too," she said. "In your way."

"Like dance therapy?" he asked.

She asked, "Is that what you were doing with . . . ?"

"Maggie Abbott," he said. "Yes. Continue it, please."

"What does your father think?" she asked.

"If it works, Pa'll try anything."

"Including a woman doctor?"

"If it works."

"Why did he take you off the case?"

"Her screams at night are terrible."

"So Hermann won," she said.

"If Hermann won," he said, "Pa would've told me to stop playing around with my"—he cleared his throat—"peculiar methods. He didn't."

In the pause, they both became more aware of the music. Jacob held out his arms, an invitation and a challenge.

"I don't dance," Miriam said. But, for the same reason she had opened the doors to the library, she approached him.

He put his right arm around her waist. Her back under his hand felt tense but supple. She wasn't wearing a corset. He blushed, not out of embarrassment, but out of joy—which surprised him. To hide his state, he pulled her closer, so she couldn't lean back to look at him. He was ashamed, not because his blush betrayed his feelings for her, but because in a doctor it seemed naive. He did not want her to think he was unprofessional.

Instead of resisting his hug, she yielded.

"Tell me what you dreamed last night," Jacob said.

"Billy goats," she said.

At the corner of her eye was a dried tear, not from sorrow but from sleep, crusty and shiny like a fleck of mica.

"Do you know the story about the three billy goats Gruff?" she asked. "How they went up into the mountains to eat and make themselves fat? They came to a bridge, and under that bridge lived a wicked troll. I was never afraid of the troll. I was terrified of the billy goats, especially the biggest billy goat, with his horns as long as spears and his hooves as big as boulders. He poked out the troll's eyes, did terrible things to him. In the book I had as a child, the billy goat's face was narrow and cruel, and he had a wispy beard that was horrible, a devil's beard. I was about two and a half, maybe three. And I was always so afraid that my father finally taught me a magic spell to chase the imaginary billy goats away: 'Billy goats begone.' After that, he said, every once in a while I used to stop whatever I was doing—playing with my doll, running around the room, eating—and whisper, 'Billy goats begone.' "

"No billy goats around here," Jacob said.

"Hermann doesn't approve of me, does he?" she asked.

"He doesn't approve of anyone," he said.

"Do you approve of me?"

"Unlike my brother," he said, "I approve of everyone."

The answer, too general, was not what she had expected or wanted.

Miriam pulled away from Jacob and stopped the record.

"I meant as a doctor," she lied.

"I'll show you around," Jacob said.

It was an apology.

She agreed, the apology accepted.

Jacob went to get their coats.

From the hall, he glanced at her. She was touching the back of her head, but the gesture was not languid enough to be primping. It was tentative, fearful. She looked, Jacob thought, like a soldier who'd just survived an attack, checking to make sure he wasn't injured.

He led her up the windy hill to the Staff House stable and introduced her to Trauma. Before descending the hill again, he waved down the road at the Director's House.

"Taboo for staff except once a year on Founder's Day," he said. "Founder's Day was Hermann's idea, as is the house being off limits to everyone but family. Ma'd love to mother everyone, staff and patients, and Pa couldn't care less about visitors. He just sits in that tower all day, trying to figure out the secret of mental health."

"Why do you always sound so smug?" she asked.

"I wish I felt smug," he said, laughing. "I thought I was being cynical."

Jacob showed her the infirmary, gymnasium, rooms for hydro-, electro-, and massage therapy, and escorted her through the wards. When they entered one room, the patients, nocturnal creatures surprised by light, scurried away, nightgowns flapping like wings. In their presence Jacob always felt like a lens that focused the sun so sharply he couldn't help burning them. In another room, a man crouched in the corner of his bed, his eyes as narrow as gun-turret slits. In a third room, a boy splayed himself against the wall like a moth. As Jacob and Miriam walked through a hall, a fat man with a white beard sidled along, whining about how badly the attendants treated him.

They left through a back door and wandered down to an iron bench overlooking the river. Jacob had forgotten his gloves, so he kept his arms crossed and his bare hands tucked in his armpits. Overhead, clouds sailed past like zeppelins.

"Are you successful here?" she asked.

"According to Hermann we are," he said. "Every year we have room for more and more patients."

"You sound like you think that's terrible," she said.

"We get rooms by adding wings," he said, "not by sending people home."

"Do you resent me for taking away your patient?" she asked.

"Yes," he said.

Although equally uncomfortable with what Jacob had admitted, they reacted in opposite ways. Miriam closed up, hunching forward, her elbows on her knees. Jacob opened up, stretching out his legs and spreading his arms along the back of the bench.

"Why is Maggie Abbott so important to you?" Miriam asked.

"Mumbo jumbo," Jacob warned.

"Why assume I'll think your theories crazy?" she asked.

"But you do," he said. "Still, since you want to hear my pitch, I might as well give you a good show."

Jacob stood and this time burlesqued not his father's lecturing style but his own, a prowl, a zoo-bred beast circling its cage, searching for an escape back to a wild it never knew. Behind him, the river scintillated. It was so bright that Jacob, striding back and forth, seemed to Miriam a featureless shadowy creature, one of the disembodied souls about which he was talking—souls that are seized by demons and dragged into infernal regions where they learn wisdom, while their bodies, abandoned on earth, hollow bags of skin, go through the motions of life skewed.

"To us they look mad," Jacob said. "But they get through it wiser and stronger. They've been on wonderful journeys."

Miriam felt his intensity as a vacuum. It was sucking him up, making him vanish into the glare of the river. It threatened to suck her up, too. She resisted the pull.

"All over the world," he continued, "you find the same thing. In Siberia, among the Yakuts. In the Pacific, among the Niue. In Uganda, among the Lotuko. I've got notebooks filled with examples. Everywhere, except among civilized nations, people we'd lock up in the Main House are revered as shamans and seers. Or feared as possessed."

"Magic and diabolism," she said. "What should we do with Maggie Abbot? Worship her or burn her at the stake?"

"Turn down the case," he said. "Let me keep working with her."

"You're medieval," she said.

"I'm not as eclectic as my father," he said. "I think there's a right way. One way."

"Your way."

"If any other way worked . . ." he said.

"Psychoanalysis," she said.

"Not by itself," he said. "It's not enough. Look, out of every ten patients, one, maybe two, go home. The rest are stranded. Like people who were on vacation behind enemy lines when the war broke out."

"And Maggie Abbott's your guinea pig," she said.

"Her soul's halfway home," he said.

She crossed one leg over the other, an aggressively modern pose. To her, it was an automatic, almost magical defense against the appeal of his theories. To him, it seemed a dismissal of everything he'd been saying.

"Do you really believe in the soul?" she asked.

"You don't?" he asked back.

"No," she said.

Jacob grabbed her shoulders. Pulling her face so close that their noses brushed, he said, "Look at me. Look into my eyes. Don't turn away. Look at me."

He shook her so violently she was scared.

"Now," he said, "damn my soul to hell."

"What?" she asked.

"Damn my soul to hell," he said. "If souls don't exist, it doesn't matter. Say it: 'Damn your soul to hell.' "

"I will not," she said.

"Say it," he said.

She twisted her shoulders. "Let me go," she said.

He tightened his grip. "You believe."

"Superstition," she said.

Suddenly, he pulled her up off the bench and kissed her. She moved her head slightly from side to side as though she were not kissing but nuzzling. Jacob had never before kissed a woman who did that. It was both erotic and innocent.

"I've wanted to kiss you ever since you bicycled up yesterday," he said.

"It's nice being adults," she said.

"So we don't have to be ashamed?" he asked.

"So we don't have to do something we don't want to do," she said. "It's late. And I'm cold." She started back to the Main House.

"Miriam," he called after her, "I love you."

Over her shoulder, she shouted, "Billy goats begone."

Chapter 14

Jacob had met Maggie Abbott in 1911, during his second year of study with James Jackson Putnam at Harvard Medical School. Putnam was an acquaintance of Maggie's husband, Baird, and from the little he saw of her in society it was obvious she needed help.

But Baird refused to admit there was anything wrong with Maggie, so Putnam asked him if he would, as a favor, rent a room to a student, Jacob. Putnam suspected that Baird admitted to himself that something was the matter with his wife, and renting a room to Jacob would allow him to accept therapy for Maggie without losing face.

Because Baird was ashamed of having Jacob there, he treated him as though he were a poor relation who had been taken in out of charity. Baird, a big man with a bluff manner, was in the habit of springing out of the parlor as Jacob was on his way up or down the stairs. He would peer earnestly into Jacob's face, ask how his studies were progressing, and, on getting a satisfactory answer, clap Jacob too hard on the back, saying, "Keep at it."

Baird was impeccably groomed and always was in a hurry, fussily consulting his pocket watch and muttering, "Oh dear, it's getting late," like the White Rabbit. When nervous, he even twitched his nose in a rabbity way. Once, half an hour after Baird had rushed from the house, Jacob saw him in the Public Garden, riding a swan boat. He sat very straight, his cane planted firmly in front of him between his legs, his gloved hands one on top of the other gripping the cane's silver knob.

Maggie was taller than her husband. Her coloring was so delicate she seemed to have been drawn in chalk, and her expression was so blurred it seemed as though the chalk had smudged. Whenever her husband spoke to her —and he spoke to her normally, not admitting even when they were alone that there was any trouble—she furrowed her brow the way someone does acknowledging the onset of a headache. Aside from that, she gave no indication of hearing.

Baird's insistence on pretending that Maggie was normal didn't seem as odd as it could have, because their relatives and friends, with one or two exceptions, conspired to maintain the fiction that Maggie was simply a dreamy sort. When they were in public, Maggie would sit or stand wherever Baird put her, staring into space and nodding her head in time to some private music. Most of the dinners they attended were, in response to her, unnaturally boisterous, so in the midst of such strange hilarity, Maggie, calmly eating and drinking what was put before her, sometimes seemed the most normal one at the table. On the few occasions when, dining at her own pace, she lagged behind or rushed ahead of everyone else, or when she ignored toasts and didn't react to the wine she spilled, it was possible for her companions to dismiss her as a mere eccentric. A couple of times an hour, Baird almost compulsively would say of Maggie, "Well, something's on her mind, for sure." Whoever was standing nearby would agree, saying, "She certainly is a deep one," or one of the other ritual phrases their circle had adopted as explanations for her behavior.

Maggie appeared continually puzzled, as though she recently had awakened to find herself transported into someone else's life. She spent her days drifting through the house, picking up and examining knickknacks as if they were clues to the identity of the person she mysteriously had become. She always ended up at the door to Jacob's room, where she stood, staring and nodding, until someone, usually Baird, with nothing more than a touch sprang some internal mechanism and she resumed her wandering. Jacob never got used to her sudden appearances, especially at night. He would wake sitting bolt upright, sure she was standing behind the closed door. After the first few times, when he flung open the door and found he was right, she was there, he never opened the door again. But, once awake, he could not fall back to sleep. He would lie, rigid with a terror he never felt for any other patient, straining to hear the creak of a loose floorboard, any hint that she was walking away.

Jacob's room had belonged to Maggie's only child, William, although nothing of his remained. Baird had crated up most of it in the cellar and destroyed the rest. Furniture, wallpaper, even the lighting fixtures had been changed. The only trace of him, which Jacob assumed Baird had missed, was on the floor of the Marie Antoinette balcony. Scratched into the stone was an obscenity.

Before her illness, Maggie had doted on William. They were inseparable. She got him tutors so he would not have to go away to school. During his lessons, she reclined on the pillows in the window seat, embroidering, and prompting him when he faltered in his recitations. No tutor lasted longer than six months.

Maggie took William everywhere with her. When she visited friends, he sat at her feet on an ottoman or cross-legged on the floor, flipping the pages of a magazine and glancing up from under his long lashes at his mother with an expression that made others in the room uneasy. In the evenings, Maggie often refused invitations so she could sit by William's bed after he went to sleep. For Maggie, the high point of every day was after dinner when she gave William his dancing lesson. Baird objected, but Maggie insisted. William had to learn to dance, and she couldn't bear the idea of his practicing at some school in the arms of a horrid little girl.

For William's fifteenth birthday, Maggie told the cook to prepare all his favorite dishes: raw oysters, consommé, grilled trout, roast saddle of lamb, asparagus, sweet corn, vanilla ice cream. She herself arranged a centerpiece of blue hydrangeas, which gave her the whimsical notion of making the celebration an old-fashioned blue dinner. Everything from the china to the table ornaments would be blue. The dessert would even be sprinkled with candied violets.

When Maggie asked Baird to bring up some of his best wine, he said, "It would be better, my dear, to have a simple party with some other children."

"He doesn't know any other children," she said.

Baird, thunderstruck, realized she was right.

At dinner, William did not touch his oysters, had only one spoonful of consommé, and picked at his trout. When the lamb was brought to the table, he mumbled, "Don't want any."

"Darling," Maggie said, "I made everything especially for you."

"Don't want any," he repeated.

Long ago, Baird had learned that Maggie would not tolerate his interference, which was what she called any attempt Baird made at disciplining William. As a result,

Baird had retreated into self-imposed blindness and deafness to his son, who—Baird knew—had become a tyrant.

But Baird loved Maggie and saw how hurt she was by William's behavior, so uncharacteristically he told his son, "Eat your dinner."

Ignoring his father and staring his mother straight in the eyes, William emptied his plate onto the floor.

Before Baird could call the maid, Maggie was around the table, on her hands and knees wiping up the mess with a napkin.

William stood on his chair, grabbed whatever he could reach, and kept dumping food onto the floor—and then onto his mother. Maggie's hair, cheeks, and blouse were covered with gravy. She did not look up at her son, and murmured over and over, "It's just a little spill."

Holding on to the back of his chair and balancing on one foot, William kicked her.

"Enough!" Baird shouted, hurling himself around the table.

He boxed his son's ear so hard the boy sprawled across the room and cracked his head against the marble fireplace.

Later that night, after his parents were asleep, William, the bandage on his head looking like a turban, ran away from home. He intended to go to South America to discover gold. He took the train to New York City, where, in a fight with a boy who tried to steal his suitcase, he was killed.

The evening Maggie heard of her son's death, Baird found her in the parlor dancing by herself. After that she never spoke, and never danced until the day Miriam came upon Jacob and her in the library.

From the very beginning Jacob had tried to reach Maggie through dancing. He played record after record, hoping one of the tunes would match the interior music to which she nodded her head. At first she ignored him, ignored the music. Then, one evening at the end of Jacob's stay in the Abbotts' house, she looked up. Just that. Nothing more. But it was a sign the therapy was working.

Baird, who was watching from the parlor door, wept. It was terrible. His tears washed away the pretense that these evenings were ordinary after-dinner musicales. He begged Jacob to stay on.

This was the job Jacob was offered in Boston and turned down.

"You have no right to abandon her," Baird told Jacob.

"Send her back to Nebraska with me," Jacob said.

But Baird refused. That would make her condition too public. Anyway, now that the breakthrough was made, it was just a matter of time. Baird would get another doctor, some expert alienist, someone with more experience than Jacob, who after all was still very young.

After Jacob left Boston, Maggie gave no more signs of coming out of her state. Baird went through doctors almost as quickly as Maggie had gone through tutors—and for similar reasons. He hovered.

Maggie's condition deteriorated. She no longer wandered through the house, but sat all day in the same chair, eyes bandaged to keep her from being overstimulated, head nodding, nodding. Just after New Year's Day, 1915, a little under a year before Miriam arrived in Galilee, Baird brought Maggie, eyes still bandaged as though she were being taken to be shot, to the Gottenberg Clinic.

Chapter 15

From the first day Miriam worked with Maggie Abbott, when Maggie had squatted, knees almost at her ears, in the corner of her room and scratched at her hair like a monkey picking fleas, Miriam had wanted to continue Jacob's dance therapy. She needed an assistant, someone who could more effectively than Jacob stand in for Maggie's son, preferably someone previously uninvolved in the case and innocent of the clinic's fratricidal politics, someone whose ideas would not get in the way of hers.

She chose Frank Kroll, a sixteen-year-old who'd been hired part-time to help Bobby Dombro, the handyman, but spent most of his afternoons at the clinic following Jacob. Hermann called him "the Sorcerer's Apprentice."

Jealous of her first case, Miriam did not want to involve Jacob, but she knew that Frank, loyal to Jacob, would not agree to help her without Jacob's approval. For three weeks, she fought her pride. The morning she decided to seek Jacob's help, she wheeled her office chair around so she could watch through the window for his arrival.

Between the Main House, where her office was, and the Director's House—beneath his bedecked apple tree—Jacob had built an Indian sweat lodge. High-domed, it seemed from a distance not primitive but futuristic, something out of a fantasy by H. G. Wells, the pitted butt-end of a half-buried projectile from space. He'd begun this project the week he'd been taken off Maggie's case, so Miriam felt some responsibility for this latest folly.

As soon as Jacob and Frank came around the Staff House stable at the top of the hill, Miriam grabbed her coat. By the time she got outside, Jacob was already squatting beside the sweat lodge, fixing a seam in the deerskin wall. He sewed with a sailmaker's needle as large as a knife. Frank stood over him, jiggling to keep warm. It was snowing, the first flurry of winter.

Ever since Jacob had kissed her at the bench overlooking the river, Miriam had avoided him when she could, and when she couldn't had rationed her conversation to a few formal phrases. Each time he hunched his shoulders, a sure sign he was about to launch into an intimate subject, Miriam excused herself. Jacob would be left thrust forward like a gargoyle.

He was knotting the gut when Miriam called. Ignoring her, he ducked into the sweat lodge. Frank, a gangly boy whose hair lay back on his head like porcupine quills, hesitated before following.

Miriam stooped to get through the low door. It was so dark she couldn't see anything. But the smell was intense: moist earth. To her, it was the smell of childhood. She remembered when she was about three, before her family had left their farm near Göllersdorf: she'd been sitting in a newly plowed field near the house when a hawk fell at her feet. The bird was dead, but when her father examined it, he found no trace of injury.

Miriam's eyes had gotten used to the dim light. In the hard-packed earth, a little off center, was a pit, over which Jacob leaned. Miriam couldn't tell what he was doing: embedding something in the dirt sides, maybe. A small rip in the roof cast a shaft of light, which looked like a glass pole, through the middle of the hut. When Jacob changed his position slightly, the pole of light shot into his head.

Without warning, he got up and plunged through the door. Frank, in agony at being left alone with Miriam, squirmed. Jacob returned, carrying a burlap bag. He knelt in the middle of the hut, again stabbed by the beam of light, and dragged from the bag handfuls of a dried plant, which he spread on the ground. The hut was filled with the smell of sage.

Whenever Jacob was rude, as he was now, Miriam was drawn to him, caught on the rough edges of his personality. Only when he was pleasant, smoothing his manners for her, was she put off. Or not so much put off as unable to get a grip on anything to like about him. The slick civilized attitudes that she demanded of others seemed in Jacob as false as the dickeys he sometimes wore instead of shirts.

He plunged through the door again and almost immediately came back wearing a demon's mask, horns corkscrewing from his forehead, slits for eyes, a beak instead of a nose, and a wide mouth with upcurving tusks.

"Now," Jacob said, his voice muffled. "What do you want?"

Miriam laughed, a little too much. She'd been more frightened than she wanted Jacob to know.

The effect was uncanny: the mask inclined in an attitude of listening; its mouth in a fixed grin; the two slits behind which Jacob's eyes darted, sunken and pale.

"You're going to use that to treat patients?" Miriam asked.

"Whatever works," he said.

Glad that the mask kept Jacob's expression hidden, Miriam said, "I need help."

The next day, Frank was so nervous as he waited for Miriam in the library that he nibbled through his lower lip and, in trying to bite off the flap of skin, tore a long bloody strip inside his mouth.

Maggie entered, with Miriam on one side and Kriger on the other. Maggie wore a black-and-white-striped shift. It was mended in dozens of places where she'd ripped it during fits. One of the orderlies had wasted the morning doing up her hair, with indifferent results. Puff curls covered her head like cocoons.

"You can go now," Miriam told Kriger.

Kriger walked a few steps to the door and stopped.

"You can go now," Miriam repeated.

"Dr. Gottenberg told me not to leave her," Kriger said.

"Jacob?" Miriam asked.

She was ready to storm his office, remind him he no longer was on Maggie's case.

"Hermann," Kriger said.

"Mrs. Abbott is my patient," Miriam said.

Kriger walked a few more steps and again stopped.

"She's strong," he said.

"So am I," Miriam said.

Miriam slid the doors shut behind him. But outside the room Kriger stood guard. Miriam heard him humming.

When she turned around, Maggie was crouched in the middle of the room. Frank, watching with big lemur eyes, held on to his seat as though the chair were about to fly through the air.

"There's nothing to be afraid of," Miriam told him.

He was waiting for some charm to arm him against Maggie's madness, his own "Billy goats begone!" Miriam wanted to tell him: *Don't give in to fear, because once you let in terror it will consume you.* The mad were frightening. It wasn't hard to see why Jacob's primitives saw them as possessed or holy. But what could slither into your soul and take root was not the fear of being infected by the evil or good that radiated from patients, but the desire to be infected.

Miriam opened the curtains. It was snowing again. Flakes swirled against the windows.

"If you weren't here," she asked Frank, "what would you be doing?"

"Cleaning up around the clinic," he said. "Or helping my dad."

"What does he do?" she asked.

"He's a printer," he said. "He doesn't work much, 'cause Mr. Loomis, who runs the newspaper, gets most of the jobs. But he's better than Mr. Loomis."

"You're proud of him?" she asked.

He said, "I don't want to be a printer."

Miriam crouched in front of Maggie.

"Come here," she told Frank.

He approached.

Miriam said, "Squat down."

When he did, she put her arm around him. The narrowness of his shoulders surprised her. How young he was. He was trembling.

"It's all right to be afraid," she said.

It was better than telling him there was nothing to fear.

"I want to introduce you," she told him.

Miriam explained to Maggie who Frank was: a friend of Jacob's and hers; he lived in town; he was going to spend some time with them after school almost every day; they would listen to music together.

Maggie didn't even blink.

"Stay here," Miriam told Frank. "Not too close."

She cranked the gramophone and put on a record.

"I'm uncomfortable," Frank said in a stage whisper.

"You can relax," Miriam said.

But he couldn't. He didn't. He sat still as a stalked animal. Or, Miriam realized, an animal that was hunting. Now she wondered not *what's he afraid of?* but *what's he looking for?*

When the session ended, Kriger took Maggie back to her room.

Frank leafed through the record album on the table. He kept blinking, trying not to cry.

"It's hard being ignored," Miriam said.

Frank asked, "What'll I do when she stops ignoring me?"

His belief in the power of his presence to cure Maggie made Miriam feel how weak her own belief was. She didn't answer him.

After Frank left, Miriam started up to the Director's House to bawl out Hermann for interfering in her case. But she no longer felt angry. She was exhausted. The first session with Frank and Maggie together had been harder than she'd expected.

The snow had stopped. In the fading light everything seemed spaced farther apart than usual. With its mantle of snow, the sweat lodge looked like an igloo. Branches creaked as though the evening were an old house that was settling.

The housekeeper let her in. She was small as a child. Her face was as shrunken as a head Miriam once saw floating in a jar in a laboratory. The housekeeper shuffled through the dark parlor to knock on the door of Hermann's study. After a moment, it opened a crack. A strip of light illuminated the old woman from the bun on the top of her head to her tiny high-buttoned shoes. A murmur. A pause. The door closed. The old woman shuffled back through the parlor to tell Miriam, "Dr. Gottenberg said he would see you at the Main House solarium in half an hour."

Miriam strode through the parlor and knocked on the door.

Hermann said, "I knew you wouldn't pay any attention."

Miriam opened the door.

Hermann sat at his desk, sideways to her. His curved back in its green silk vest made him look like a beetle.

"Obviously, you're angry," he said, glancing down his nose at a piece of paper. "Don't mind me if I keep on working."

Hermann's presence was like an animal trap. You could slip right in, but the door worked only one way. Once inside, it was impossible to escape. As usual, Miriam felt caught within his view of the world. She saw herself as he saw her: a new, insecure colleague, overreacting to unintentional slights and trying too aggressively to stake out a position in the clinic's hierarchy.

"You know why I'm here," she said.

"I don't want to deprive you of the pleasure of telling me," he said.

"Leave me alone," she said, sounding as she had at sixteen.

"I've hardly talked to you since you arrived," he said. "How alone do you want to be?"

"That's not what I mean," she said. "Mrs. Abbott belongs to me."

"She doesn't belong to anyone," he said. "What you mean is, she's your responsibility. You're wrong. She's the clinic's responsibility."

"The clinic entrusted me, not you, with her care," she said.

"No one here, particularly a new doctor, works without supervision," he said.

"I'll keep you informed about everything I do," she said. "When your father decides I'm not doing an adequate job, I'll leave the case to someone else. Until then, not you, not Jacob, not even your father has the right to undermine my authority with the staff."

Hermann grunted. "I'll talk to Kriger," he said.

Miriam hadn't expected him to give in so easily. She was halfway down the hill to the Main House, crunching through the snow in the dark, before she realized she felt cheated—and conned, as if Hermann had given Kriger the orders only so he could prove his gallantry by rescinding them.

Chapter 16

For three months, through Christmas and into the new year, every weekday after school Frank sat cross-legged in front of Maggie while Miriam played music on the gramophone and talked about what they were all doing. Her manner was factual, almost dull—"Now I'm looking through the albums for a record; now I'm choosing a record; now I'm putting the record on"—as though the very banality of their routine might coax Maggie out of her shell.

In mid-March, on a sunny, mild day, Miriam had just put on a Strauss waltz, her own favorite, when Frank noticed that Maggie was staring at him, really looking at him. He was just about to tell Miriam, when Maggie sprang forward and clawed his face.

Frank threw himself backward, his cheeks bloody.

A doctor named Bruges, who'd been passing by in the hall as Frank screamed, opened the library doors and stuck in his head.

"Get out," Miriam said.

Bruges gazed at Maggie, who was on her knees, examining her hands.

"Get out!" Miriam yelled.

Bruges shut the doors.

Miriam knelt in front of Maggie. Keeping up a soothing patter, she gestured for Frank to approach. When he did, she pulled him into a kneeling position next to her.

Maggie's eyes flicked from one to the other. Then she sank back. Her eyes went dead.

After Kriger took Maggie back to her room, Miriam asked Frank, "Do you want to quit?"

"Should I?" he asked.

Miriam was surprised by the directness of his question. Most of the time, Frank sidled through conversations. When Miriam first met him, she'd thought he was furtive. Now she suspected he simply found that what could be said in words was too narrow for what he wanted to express. For him, talking was like trying to squeeze through a half-opened door.

"I want you to stay," she said.

He grinned.

"It's the first time she's ever done something except sit there," he said.

The next day, Frank didn't show up. He'd never before missed a session. Had he decided to quit after all? Miriam considered the effects Frank's absence might have on Maggie. She picked at the cuticle of her index finger, something she hadn't done for years.

During the session, she felt the beginning of a headache, more like an itch she couldn't scratch than a pain. She told Maggie she didn't know where Frank was, promised to find out, discussed what had happened the previous day, keeping the description matter-of-fact, and played records. Maggie showed no sign of missing Frank.

When the hour was up, Miriam eagerly slid open the doors for Kriger, who led Maggie away. Uncharacteristically, Miriam didn't straighten up the room. She hurried through the patients' wing of the Main House, looking for Jacob.

She found him in the Turkish bath. The big white tiles on the walls were beaded with condensation. The marble floor was slippery. Along one side of the room were half a dozen wicker chaise longues in which women lay swathed in damp white sheets. A female attendant stood behind one of them, rubbing cream into her temples. Jacob stood next to another, jotting in a small notebook. His face was red and glistening, his beard wet, and his wool suit limp.

"Have you seen Frank today?" she asked him.

"No," he said.

"Could you take me into town?" she asked.

Jacob gestured toward his patients. "I can't neglect them," he said.

By the time Miriam had changed into her knickerbocker suit and gotten her bicycle from the Staff House cellar, the inside of her head felt sheathed in glass. A bump and it would shatter. She pedaled off, holding the handlebars with one hand, pressing the heel of her other hand into her left eye to ease her headache.

Frank lived in the outskirts of Galilee in a tall and narrow house, which looked as though it were about to topple. The front door, a foot off the ground, had no steps leading up to it.

As Miriam bicycled up, three children, all under ten, stopped running around the patch of dirt that served as a yard. They stood, immobile and tense, like kids playing freeze tag, squinting against the dust which the wind whipped into their faces. When Miriam dismounted, they edged together. The two younger children, girls, wore white aprons over dresses as purple as eggplant. The boy wore a black cap with a visor, a gray-and-white-checked shirt, white suspenders, black pants, and high-laced work boots.

When Miriam knocked on the side door, the children scattered, released from their spell by the noise. Frank's mother, Diana Kroll, opened the door.

Her black hair, massed on her head, looked, Miriam thought, not sloppy but magnificent. Her face was so white her features seemed carved from bone. Her eyes were as black as her hair. Miriam was startled by how vivid she was.

After Miriam explained who she was, Diana turned her back on Miriam. She vigorously stirred something in an iron pot.

"May I come in?" Miriam asked, entering.

"You will anyway," Diana said.

Miriam blushed. She was already closing the door behind her.

"I'm sorry Frank got hurt yesterday," Miriam said.

Diana threw the spoon into the sink so hard it flipped over the side onto the floor.

Miriam picked it up.

"I'm not so dumb," Diana said, and she slammed from the room. Miriam put the spoon in the sink. She went to the door Diana had banged shut. It opened. Miriam faced a short old man. His bald head was speckled with liver spots. He had a mustache so long it covered his mouth. And each eyebrow, tufted and prickly as a burr, grew in a single clump.

"Go away," he said. He had a Slavic accent.

"Where is Frank?" Miriam asked.

"Go away," he said.

"Is he all right?" she asked.

"My son came home last night with blood on his face," he said.

"I want to explain," she said.

He threw his hands into the air as though he were tossing confetti.

"Go away!" he shouted. "Go away! Go away!"

Miriam backed out of the house, almost falling from the high sill. Frank's father stood at the door, chanting, "Go away. Go away. Go away," until she mounted her bicycle and pedaled out of the yard.

Miriam's headache was worse. It felt as if fragments of her skull had been ripped away like pieces of fingernail, exposing the quick beneath. She could never make it back to the clinic. She wobbled on her bicycle through town to Jacob's house.

No one was home, but the house was not locked. Miriam wrestled her bicycle up the front porch steps, propped it against the porch railing, and staggered into the parlor, where she collapsed into a chair.

A noise woke her. Water running. No, someone pouring something. She opened her eyes. Jacob was putting an amber-colored bottle, whiskey, on a table.

"May I?" Miriam asked.

Jacob handed her his glass.

"I was going to kiss you awake like Sleeping Beauty," he said.

Miriam took a gulp of whiskey. She felt as though someone had slit her with a razor from under her chin to her belly button, the path the liquor burned.

She took a second and third gulp, and with each the initial effects dulled, until by the fourth gulp she hardly felt the whiskey go down. She finished the glass and coughed. The lights in the room were cozier, the chair more enveloping, the room, the whole house more inviting. She closed her eyes, felt as though she were tipping backward, opened them, and was surprised to see Jacob still there.

"You don't fool me, Jacob," she said.

She pushed herself out of the chair. Crossing to Jacob, she kissed him on the lips so hard their teeth hit.

Jacob grabbed her waist, half to steady her and half to push her away.

"Don't be like that," she said.

She closed her eyes and puckered her lips. Jacob didn't kiss her. She opened her eyes.

"Why won't you when you want to when you can?" she asked. "I'll show you."

Fumbling, she unbuttoned the top button of her blouse.

"Miriam," Jacob said.

She fumbled with the second button.

"Stop," Jacob said.

She fumbled with the third button. A V of her vertically ribbed union suit was exposed.

"I'll leave," Jacob said.

"I'll wait for you," Miriam said.

She had trouble with the fourth button, so she ripped the blouse apart. Buttons popped off. Her union suit was sleeveless and edged with mercerized lace. Between her breasts was a sewed-on blue bow.

"I wish you weren't drunk," Jacob said.

"Gift horses," she said.

"What?" he asked.

"Don't look into their mouths," she said. "Remember, curiosity killed the cat."

Jacob hooked his finger under her right shoulder strap and pulled it down, uncovering her breast. They both looked at it, surprised.

Clasping his hands behind his back, Jacob asked, "Miriam, will you marry me?"

"No," she said.

"How can you say no?" he said.

Miriam picked up the bottle and took a swig.

"Don't get drunker," Jacob said.

He grabbed the bottle. Whiskey poured down her chin.

"Bastard," she said. "Give it."

Jacob sighed and handed her the bottle.

She drank and said, "I want you to talk to Frank's father."

"What?" Jacob said.

"I want you to talk to Frank's father," she said.

"Miriam," Jacob said, "I just asked you to marry me."

"I want you to convince him to let Frank come back," she said.

"Marry me," Jacob said.

"No," Miriam said.

Jacob left the room. Alone, Miriam snapped her union suit back over her breast and bitterly said, "Psychoanalyst triumphs again."

Chapter 17

Miriam woke at dawn in an unfamiliar bed. She was dressed as she had been when she'd passed out. Jacob must have carried her upstairs to a guest room. She expected to be sick after the previous night's binge, but she was merely thirsty. And she had an almost hallucinatory clarity of vision. She pinned her ripped blouse together and set off on her bicycle for the clinic. The air smelled as fresh as the inside of a cucumber. At one farm she passed, a rooster was perched on the roof of the barn, its chest out and head back as it crowed and crowed.

She reached her room in the Staff House without encountering anyone. After washing and changing, she hurried to the Director's House. Hermann opened the front door, pushed her backward onto the porch, and shut the door behind him.

"I don't want the Director to hear," he said.

His chest heaved; the skin around his mouth was taut; his eyes were bloodshot.

"I know where you were last night," he said.

"Did Jacob send out a memo?" she asked.

"You don't deny it," he said.

"Why should I?"

"It looks bad for the clinic."

"I'm sick of hearing about the clinic," she said.

"You have to be above reproach," he said.

"Hermann," she said, "will you do me a favor? The boy who's been helping me on the Abbott case. Talk to his father."

"He shouldn't be helping you," Hermann said.

"You're such a stick," she said, brushing past him.

"You used to like me," he said.

That was so unlike him, so pathetic, Miriam's eyes filled with tears; but she slammed the door behind her.

Abraham came out of the dining room. He wore a green robe with gold patterns: tridents, crescents, and triangles. The sleeves, rolled back, bared his forearms, which were hairless and as yellow as old ivory. His beard, freshly washed, looked silky. Above his beard, his cheeks were plump as a baby's. The robe had an attached hood, which framed his face and peaked as stiffly as a wizard's conical cap.

Merlin, Miriam thought.

Which was probably the effect he was trying to create. As he grew older, he got more theatrical.

"Excuse me for barging in, Dr. Gottenberg," she said, "but I need your help."

"After I dress, you can tell me about it," he said.

Halfway up the stairs, he leaned over the banister to say, "You're right. He is a stick."

Solomon Kroll, Frank's father, was born in Odessa in 1875. He was the oldest of eight children, a bookish boy, who, proud of his name, used to hold court in his imagination, resolving make-believe disputes with clever and just solutions; but whenever he tried to mediate among his squabbling siblings, they jeered at him. He learned that wisdom without authority is despised.

In 1890, when Solomon was fifteen, his father, Aaron, died. He was sitting in a chair, taking his usual after-dinner nap, a handkerchief covering his face, when Solomon noticed that the cloth, instead of dimpling in and out over his mouth, was still. Solomon ran into the kitchen, where his Uncle Samuel, a cigar sticking out from the corner of his mouth, one eye squinting in the smoke, caressed his mother's back. For a dozen years Uncle Samuel had flirted with Solomon's mother. All during that time Solomon's mother had pretended he wasn't serious, slapping away his hands.

Solomon said, "Papa's dead."

His mother and uncle ran into the other room, hurrying as people do when faced with the leisure of death. Samuel flipped off the handkerchief and held the glass face of a pocket watch up to Aaron's mouth.

Uncle Samuel was an agnostic who had rejected the comforts but not the superstitions of religion, so he felt he had to prove he wasn't intimidated by the corpse. He swaggered, told jokes, and became hysterically flirtatious with Solomon's mother.

Whenever Solomon was frightened, particularly by behavior he couldn't understand, he took refuge in piety.

"You're breaking God's law," he told his uncle.

"This is God's law," Samuel said. He picked up Solomon and stuck his face right in his dead father's. Solomon noticed with disgust that the inside of his father's open mouth was dry as velvet.

"Look closely, little rabbi," Samuel said. He threw the boy onto the corpse. Solomon's face smacked so hard against his father's bared teeth that he cut his cheek.

Solomon learned the lesson well. He lost his faith, although for the sake of his mother, brothers, and sisters he continued to go through the motions until he ran away in 1896, to America, to New York City.

He shared a room on Grand Street with a Lithuanian Jew named Lake, a printer who taught him the trade, but because Solomon couldn't get into the printers' union, he couldn't find a job. When the union went on strike, Solomon became a scab. Every day he walked in the shadows of the Third Avenue El to the Astoria Press. The company pirated books. In the glare of a green-shaded lamp, Solomon scanned the copy he was setting, trying not to get interested in the story, Kipling's "The Brushwood Boy." Swiftly, he clicked type into his composing stick. When he left the factory, striking workers screamed at him. They spit into his face and said, "We'll kill you."

Solomon bought a revolver, an old Frontier Colt with a sawed-off barrel.

During his second week on the job, when he came out of the factory, a beefy red-haired man, about his own age, embraced him. At first Solomon thought it was a friend or relative from Russia; but as the man's grip tightened, he whispered hateful names into Solomon's ear. Solomon understood he was being attacked.

"Look at her," the red-haired man said, pointing his chin at a woman holding a child near them. "And look at the baby. They haven't eaten in three days because of you."

Yes, Solomon said to himself, he's right.

At the same time, he struggled with the red-haired man. Afraid of being killed, he twisted the gun around in his pocket so it pointed at the man's belly and pulled the trigger. The shot was the loudest sound he'd ever heard. His thigh was scorched. The red-haired man slumped. Now it was Solomon who held him, one arm around his waist. He looked over the dead man's shoulder at the dead man's wife and daughter, who did not yet realize what had happened.

Solomon ran. He hid for two weeks, long enough to learn the name and address of the man's widow. After that, wherever he went, from town to town, farther and farther west, he anonymously sent half of what he earned to her, until she moved or died and the envelopes came back marked "Addressee unknown."

That sin, the murder he'd committed, sparked in him sin's anodyne. If he'd lost one faith in his uncle's grip, he found another in the grip of the red-haired stranger. Not the Judaism of his forebears, but Christianity. Not the angry, jealous, vindictive God who tested Abraham, sent flood and fire to destroy the wicked, and punished Job to prove a point; but the merciful, forgiving God who sacrificed His Son to save a sinful world. This—in Solomon's rude theology—was what he worshipped: mercy.

Solomon settled in Galilee for no particular reason. It was where he happened to stop. When he met Diana, who was working in her father's dry goods store, his body became quicksand for his soul. Every night in his imagination, she flounced as nearly naked as his mind could make her without losing the thrill of mystery. When he pictured her completely stripped, she seemed as innocent as Eve before the Fall; she needed some lace to tickle his lust. He believed a sin in thought was equal to a sin in deed, so he courted Diana not out of love but to make himself an honest man.

Diana was intrigued by this intense stranger. She never loved him, but finally she couldn't help reflecting back to him some of his passion for her. When her parents refused to give their consent to the match, Diana seduced Solomon in the sweet-smelling field behind her parents' house. She lay on her back, her skirt bunched around her waist, the grass prickling her buttocks and thighs. Her eyes were filled with stars, which pulsed in time to the beating of her blood. As he entered her, he groaned as though some membrane in him were breaking. His last resistance to God. Until that time, although fiercely religious, he hadn't joined a church, believing that he needed no intermediary between him and God, the heretic's pride. Now he realized that his will was weak. He needed the strength of a church to force the gates of his heart and let Christ enter. And he understood that outside the church he had no protection against his worship becoming idiosyncratic. Just as the sin of murder had led him to God, the sin of lust led him to Rome. He converted to Catholicism, Diana's faith. The Church welcomed him, not just for his soul, but for his physical strength, because in Galilee, as in many plains states towns, the Catholic Church was often attacked by the Ku Klux Klan.

Diana's face, hovering in a window, merged with a reflection of a tree branch, which seemed to grow from her head like an antler. Solomon opened the door and said to Miriam, "Back you come. For what? To understand more how much we don't want you here?"

Abraham said, "We don't want to hurt your son."

"Want? Not want?" Solomon said. "He gets hurt. And not just his face. In his heart, too. Home he comes and lectures me on savage gods; idolatry that never in my house before was preached. Eagle gods and gods in trees and gods with wolf heads and no love in their breasts for mankind. Who will save him from the damnation your son Jacob, forgive me, Dr. Gottenberg, is leading him to?"

"My son's not a preacher, but a doctor," Abraham said. "He leads no one to damnation. He's interested in other religions because he wants to understand what men believe so he can help the troubled."

"Only God can help the troubled," Solomon said.

"Come back with me," Abraham said. "I'll show you how we help."

"My son tells me the things you do," Solomon said. "The dancing tricks and talking cures."

"The patients feel better after talking to us," Abraham said.

"Confession belongs to the priest," Solomon said, "not the doctor."

"The priest can't heal their minds," Abraham said.

"The doctor cannot save their souls," Solomon said. "God's judgment we see in madness. You can do one thing only with your healing of minds: turn lunatics away from knowing the sins that corrupt their souls. By helping them, as you call it, you damn them—just like you damn my son."

"No," Abraham said. "The mad are not sinful, or no more than we all are. They're sick. They have no choice. They're driven to do the things they do by their pasts—"

"Their sins," Solomon said.

"They're not responsible for what they are or what they do," Abraham said. "Like the woman who scratched your son. She couldn't help it."

"A choice she had," Solomon said. "She and all of us. Right over wrong, we choose. God over Satan."

"You're harsh to blame her," Abraham said.

"God's judgment is harsher," Solomon said.

"To understand is to forgive," Abraham said.

"Dr. Gottenberg," Solomon said, "you are, I think, a good man. But you are not, I think, a godly man."

"Frank is helping us with a heroic task," Abraham said. "We're learning why people act as they do—an understanding we can use to reshape man's idea of what he is."

"Yes, yes, heroic," Solomon said. "But what heroic really is, is not the special, not your reshaping of man's idea of what he is. Man is man. But the ordinary. The man who at four o'clock wakes up to work for eighteen hours to feed and shelter his wife and children; that is heroic. The woman who raises twelve children without complaining and a cheerful, healthy home gives them; that is heroic. Heroism I heard a lot about in Europe, revolutions and your reshaping of men. But heroism is not in revolutions, not in revolutions from guns and not in revolutions from books. Heroism is a man's struggle to get through the day doing no evil, causing no harm."

Abraham and Miriam climbed into the buggy.

"You will promise if my son comes to your hospital, you will send him home?" Solomon asked.

"He's past the age of reason," Abraham said. "By your own logic, he must make his own choices."

"You cannot come between a father and his son," Solomon said.

"The sanity of a woman is at stake," Abraham said.

"At stake is my son's soul," Solomon said.

"I'm sorry, Mr. Kroll," Abraham said, "but I don't believe that. And I won't trade a woman's mind for a superstition."

"You are a selfish man," Solomon said.

"I know," Abraham said. "But I'm selfish for others."

"May God forgive you," Solomon said.

Abraham snapped the reins and said, "Amen."

Chapter 18

When Miriam arrived in the library the next day, Frank was there, dressed in his Sunday best: a brown checked knee-pants suit, black calf-length stockings held up by garters that were not quite hidden, and ankle shoes made of two tones of leather, one dark and one light—"Holstein shoes," the boys in Galilee called them with contempt. On his lap he held a golf-style cap made of the same muddy check as his suit. As soon as he saw Miriam, he jumped up.

"I ran away," he said.

"You'd better go back," Miriam said.

"What about Mrs. Abbott?" he asked.

The library doors opened. Kriger guided Maggie into the room. When she saw Frank, she held out her arms. At first Miriam and Frank were too surprised to do anything. Maggie raised two fingers, three fingers, five fingers, then held out her arms again.

"Dance with her," Miriam told Frank.

"What if she doesn't—" he started to say.

But Maggie floated into his embrace.

Miriam put a waltz on the gramophone.

"She's leading," Frank said.

Round and round they went. The record ended.

Maggie sat on a chair and folded her hands in her lap, as though doing so were as ordinary as in truth it was.

"Mrs. Abbott," Miriam said, "do you understand me?"

Maggie didn't respond.

But when Miriam started her daily monologue, caring and coaxing, Maggie's right eye twitched. The more Miriam talked, the more out-of-control the twitching became. Instead of a sign of insanity, Miriam, under Jacob's influence, believed it was a sign of health. Madness, Miriam thought, was total, irresistible control, a tyrant subjugating a state. Health was, paradoxically, being out of control—spontaneity. Maggie's twitching was the revolt of reason against insanity.

If only Maggie could trust herself to be out of control. Like Christ's paradox: you have to lose your life to gain your life. You have to give up control to gain real control, to be sane. Maybe Abraham and Solomon were talking about the same thing without realizing it. Sanity, grace . . .

After Kriger took Maggie back to her room, Miriam ran outside to tell Jacob what had happened.

Jacob was digging a trench a half dozen yards from his lodge. His coat was off. The back of his vest was so sweaty, his suspenders were outlined in the cloth. At her voice, he looked up, but his gaze slid over her head and to the right—at what? Miriam glanced behind her. Down the hill from the Staff House came Solomon. Like his son, he was dressed in his Sunday best: a black wool suit, a black dogskin coat, and a derby with a rolled brim. One hand was flat on the top of his hat to keep it from flying off as he ran; the other hand was pointing at Frank.

"I see you!" he shouted.

Frank backpedaled a few steps, but Miriam advanced. Ignoring Miriam, Solomon glared at his son. He was breathing heavily. He took his hand from his hat and placed it over his heart. His other hand, still pointing, shook.

"Come," he told Frank.

"Mr. Kroll," Miriam said, "I have to tell you something."

"Come," Solomon said to his son.

"Papa," Frank said, "you can't."

"Can't, can I?" Solomon said. The hand that had been pointing became a fist, which he shook in Frank's face. " 'Honor thy father and thy mother: that *thy* days may be long upon the land which the Lord thy God giveth thee.' "

"Oh, Papa," Frank said.

"Papa me no Papa," Solomon said. "God gave Moses the commandment. 'Honor thy father and thy mother.' Come."

Jacob ran from his trench. Hermann was running from the Main House.

"I know he disobeyed you," Miriam said, "but you have to understand."

"Woman, keep quiet!" Solomon shouted at Miriam.

"Don't yell at her," Hermann said.

"Hold it," Jacob said. Catching up to Hermann, he put a restraining hand on his shoulder.

Hermann whipped around.

"Don't interfere," he told Jacob.

"You're the one interfering," Jacob said. "Don't you understand what's happening?"

"One of our doctors is being abused by a stranger," Hermann said.

"Stranger, am I?" Solomon said. "But not so strange you can turn my son against me."

"Frank's his son," Jacob said.

"You're siding with him?" Miriam said.

"You hear him," Solomon told Miriam, shaking his fist. "Even he says you have no right."

"Don't raise your hand to her," Hermann said. He grabbed Solomon's wrist.

Jacob grabbed Hermann's arm.

The three of them struggled, staggering a few steps in one direction, a few steps in another direction. At last, Hermann released Solomon's wrist and swung at Jacob, slugging him on the side of the neck.

Jacob fell. "We'll finish this later," he said.

"Oh, Christ," Hermann said.

" 'Thou shalt not take the name of the Lord thy God in vain; for the Lord will not hold him guiltless that taketh His name in vain,' " Solomon said to Hermann.

But no one paid any attention to him. His complaint about Frank had been replaced by some conflict between the Gottenberg brothers, which he did not understand.

"I am going home," he told Frank. "If you do not come, you no longer are my son."

He started up the hill. Frank ran after him, not because of his threat, but because he was embarrassed at having witnessed the fight between Jacob and Hermann.

"You're ridiculous," Hermann told Jacob.

"Tomorrow morning," Jacob said.

"Don't play his game," Miriam said.

"Tomorrow morning," Hermann agreed.

"Clowns," Miriam said.

But at five-thirty the next morning, she was watching from a window in the Main House library when Jacob and Hermann, fists up, circled each other. She went into the Main House kitchen, grabbed two of the biggest knives she could find, and brought them out.

"If you're going to fight," she told them, "fight."

She threw the knives on the ground and walked away.

Embarrassed, Jacob and Hermann watched her go.

Hermann picked up Jacob's coat and handed it to him.

Jacob picked up the knives and followed Miriam into the Main House library. He dropped them on the table near the window where she stood.

"You think I betrayed you yesterday, don't you?" he said.

"You betrayed yourself, your own methods," she said. "Maggie danced with Frank."

"And you want to save her," he said, "even if it means sacrificing Frank and his father."

"I thought you believed in doing whatever was necessary," she said.

"I believe in not having illusions," he said.

That afternoon, Frank was waiting for Miriam in the library again.

"Didn't you hear what your father said yesterday?" Miriam asked. She was angry at Frank for disobeying his father, but glad he had.

"I'll go if you want me to," Frank said.

"Stay," Miriam said.

That afternoon, Maggie danced again. And her silence had a new quality. She seemed not so much withdrawn as thoughtful.

At the end of the second waltz, Frank for the first time since he'd been coming to the sessions felt comfortable enough to be playful. He stepped back, bowed. Maggie threw back her head and howled. It was not the uncanny, soulless scream she used to make at night, but a howl of consciousness, a newborn's bawl, if an infant came into the world knowing all the grief it would later experience. Tears streamed down her cheeks, and through her tears she looked around the room as if seeing it for the first time.

Miriam saw her glance land on the knives Jacob had left on the table by the window. She started toward them at the same moment Maggie did. Grabbing one by the blade, Miriam sliced her palm.

Maggie got the other knife by the handle. With a single sweeping gesture, she plunged it into her breast. For a moment, there was no blood. Even though she saw the hilt of the knife sticking out of Maggie's chest, Miriam had the crazy hope that she was unhurt. Then a spot of blood dilated like an opening iris.

Maggie slumped to the floor. Miriam did what she could, but Maggie had died almost instantly. As orderlies carried the body away, Miriam took Frank in her arms. He buried his face against her shoulder.

Chapter 19

To distract Miriam after Maggie's suicide, Abraham sent her to Lincoln to lobby at the legislature for state support for the Nebraska Committee for Mental Hygiene, an organization Abraham recently founded and modeled after the National Committee for Mental Hygiene, which had been started seven years earlier in the East.

"You don't have to go," Jacob told Miriam. He had caught her in her office, where she was packing.

"I'm not running away," she said.

Jacob watched her open and close desk drawers, sort papers into piles, weigh a book in each hand as though judging from their heft which would bring more pleasure. As he left, he asked, "Can I meet you in Lincoln?"

She didn't answer.

In Lincoln, Miriam was startled by the clangor of trolleys and grinding gears of automobiles, the shrill voices of people, the long, determined strides of pedestrians. She'd forgotten how quiet Galilee was.

Abraham had reserved a room for her in the new Metropolitan Hotel. It had a brass bed that gleamed. From the ceiling hung a chandelier with frosted shades, etched with an ivy design. She even had a private bathroom with a toilet tank made of oak.

Miriam cranked the telephone on the wall (another luxury that made her uneasy) and told the desk she wanted to move into less lavish quarters. The clerk put the manager on the line.

"I have instructions here saying I can give you a better room but not something worse," the manager said. "Whoever made your reservations wants you to be comfortable."

Furious at Abraham for anticipating her reaction, Miriam said, "Give me the best room in the hotel."

They moved her into a four-room suite.

For three weeks, she made the rounds of legislators, accosting some in their lairs, tracking others to parties where she wasted her charms. The politicians were indulgent, treating her as though she were merely one more eccentric, a suffragette or a matron intoxicated with prohibition.

The night before she left Lincoln, she woke to hear someone breathing heavily in the dark of her bedroom. She was terrified. A tingling spread from behind her ears across the back of her head. She expected the breathing to vanish as she roused herself. Instead, it grew clearer. Miriam couldn't control her trembling. Suddenly, she knew—without knowing how—that whoever or whatever was breathing was perched on the wall above her head. She closed her eyes.

She knew—also without knowing how—that she was being visited by a ghost.

"Maggie," Miriam said.

There was no answer, but the breathing grew more labored. It was terrible, the sound of someone suffocating.

"I'm sorry," Miriam said.

The breathing stopped.

Miriam opened her eyes. On the wall above her head, she saw a flicker. And she felt a sharp slap on her left cheek.

Jumping from bed, she turned on the light and ran to a mirror. The slapped cheek was red.

She spent the rest of the night rigid in a chair, all the lights in her suite lit.

In the morning, she convinced herself that the breathing had been an auditory hallucination; the flicker, a disturbance of the optic nerve; and the slap, autosuggestion.

A month after Miriam returned to Galilee, she and Jacob were sitting on the hill overlooking the Main House, watching Kriger give a piggyback ride to one of Hermann's patients, Louise McGraw. Louise was a hysteric who'd lost the use of her legs the week her brother married one of her college classmates. Most of the other patients disliked her and joked about how she was always talking about "slimming." She was so robust that her parents refused to believe she couldn't walk. The first doctors they brought in accused her of shamming to get attention.

She certainly wanted attention, and she got it by bearing her hysterical paralysis with a fortitude that demanded admiration. She was a model patient, the cheerful-in-the-face-of-adversity patient, the patient who is continually forgiving her family for her misfortune, as though they conspired to convince her of the paralysis and she went along with it so their malice would not be revealed. She smiled too much.

Miriam identified with Louise's false bravery and appreciated the solidity of her body, the broadness of her shoulders and hips, which gave her the look of being aligned with some elemental force of the planet. She seemed both ancient and new, a statue of a Greek goddess which had been just unearthed. And despite her cultivated martyrdom, Miriam even liked her. More than once Miriam noticed that just when Louise was at her sunniest, her face betrayed the panic of an actress who has come to the end of a play and, trapped on stage because the curtain doesn't descend, is struggling to keep the audience entertained. Behind the false martyrdom was a real martyrdom.

Lately, Kriger had begun spending a lot of his off-duty time with Louise. Her legs tucked under his arms, he galloped across the lawn. Instead of wearing her usual forced smile, Louise was radiant. Whenever Kriger stopped to catch his breath, she shouted, "More!"

"Kriger's doing more for her than Hermann," Jacob said.

Just then, Hermann appeared in the doorway of the Main House.

"Kriger!" he shouted.

Kriger loped to Hermann. Hands in his trouser pockets, Hermann rocked up and down on the balls of his feet as he scolded. Kriger's head was bowed, but he wore a piratical grin. He looked as if any moment he might seize Hermann by the throat.

"He's jealous of Kriger's success," Jacob told Miriam.

"Why do you always think the worst about him?" she asked.

"You've been defending him an awful lot lately," he said.

"We can't have romances between staff and patients," she said.

"You're even beginning to sound like him," he said.

Miriam went down the hill and took up a position beside Hermann.

* * *

That night, pounding woke Jacob. Disoriented from his dreams, he tried to identify the sound. A horse kicking in its stall? A branch knocking against the roof? The obvious explanation dawned last: someone at the front door.

Jacob flipped back the covers. Swinging his legs around, he grunted—which surprised him. He never before noticed himself grunting with normal physical effort. In fact, he was arrogant about what good shape he was in.

He slept naked, so he put on the buffalo fur coat he used as a bathrobe and lumbered out of the bedroom. When he opened the front door, he found Miriam, fist raised, about to knock again.

"Kriger's run off with Louise," she said. "I thought you might have an idea where they went."

"I had nothing to do with it," he said.

"I wasn't accusing you," she said.

Jacob's coat was unbuttoned. Simultaneously, they both became aware of his nakedness. Jacob clutched the coat closed.

"I want to get them back to the clinic before Hermann finds out," Miriam said. "Otherwise, he'll sack Kriger."

"Kriger's grandfather had a farm out in Indian Orchard," Jacob said. "It's been abandoned for years."

Miriam started down the porch steps.

"I'll go with you," Jacob said.

He ran in to get dressed.

The moon was high, the landscape luminous. They turned onto the road to Indian Orchard, leaving behind the shaded neighborhood streets and heading into open country. Both were thinking about Jacob's nakedness when he'd opened the door. At last, Miriam asked, "What if I'd been someone else?"

"If you'd been someone else," Jacob said, "I would have wondered, 'What if it had been Miriam?' "

Miriam handled the reins. Jacob smoked and let the swaying carriage tranquilize him. He recalled the time his father returned from Freud's lecture in Worcester and took Hermann and him to the Stutz farm. Everything that had happened since seemed so fated he felt he could have predicted it if he'd just been more clearheaded. Knowing the future seemed as simple as rousing oneself from a stupor.

"How will we think about these days thirty years from now?" Jacob asked.

"You mean, will things that seem important now still seem important then?" Miriam asked back.

That wasn't what Jacob meant.

"What things?" he asked.

Miriam did not elaborate.

To get to the abandoned farm, they had to leave the main road and bump over an overgrown path. Grass scratched the underside of the wagon's floorboards.

Miriam stopped far enough from the farmhouse so Kriger and Louise would not hear them. She and Jacob climbed down and swished through the waist-high grass to the house. One downstairs room was lit. Jacob and Miriam peered in.

Kriger sat on a stool that was too small. Beside him, on a couch which was spilling most of its stuffing, reclined Louise, a red blanket tucked around her legs. On the floor nearby was a willow basket they'd used as a picnic hamper and the remains of a meal.

"What are we waiting for?" Jacob whispered to Miriam.

Kriger left the room for a moment. While he was gone, Louise leaned her head back against the sofa and smiled.

"They won't be missed till morning," Miriam said. "Let's give them a little longer."

Jacob and Miriam went back to the wagon. The horse looked up and lowered its head again to chomp grass. They climbed into the wagon bed and sat side by side. Miriam leaned her head against Jacob's shoulder. He put his arm around her.

When he unbuttoned her blouse, he discovered that she wasn't wearing her union suit but a silk brassiere.

"You knew," he said.

They undressed. Jacob spread out the coach blanket, and they lay down. In the moonlight her skin looked downy, as if she were covered with tiny feathers.

After they made love, Jacob dozed—or thought he dozed. And he woke—or thought he woke—realizing that Miriam had been talking to him. He was still lying on top of her. He pushed himself up and asked, "What did you just say?"

Impatiently, she said, "Don't make me repeat it."

"What did you just say?" he demanded.

But he knew. He'd heard the first time.

She covered her eyes with an arm and said, "Hermann asked me to marry him, and I accepted."

Jacob refused to attend the ceremony. Hermann wheedled and threatened. How would Jacob's absence look to the guests? Jacob shrugged.

When Hermann, Miriam, and the wedding party returned to the clinic from church, they saw what looked like an old man standing under Jacob's apple tree, holding a bouquet of flowers. When the old man approached, Miriam said, "My God, it's Jacob!"

Jacob's head was shaved. His bald dome with its hollows and bumps looked like a dented metal cap.

"I'll never forgive you for this," Hermann said.

Jacob handed the bouquet to Miriam.

A few in the crowd massed on the hillside behind Hermann and Miriam snickered. Hermann pulled Miriam into the Main House, where the reception was to be held.

As Jacob's hair grew back, he looked like one of the patients in the violent ward. He and Hermann avoided each other. When they were forced into contact, Hermann unconsciously twisted his wedding ring on his finger, as Jacob stared, convinced his brother was doing it on purpose to remind him of the marriage.

Hermann and Miriam moved into the Director's House with Abraham and Rosa. One autumn afternoon, Miriam was reading in the parlor when Rosa fluttered in.

"Worse than children," she said. "Maybe you can stop them. I just don't understand. In the middle of the quadrangle, too."

Miriam ran onto the front porch. Down the hill, near the sweat lodge, Jacob and Hermann were fighting. Hermann swung at Jacob, who, ducking, slipped behind him and grabbed him in a headlock. He squeezed until Hermann sagged.

"Let him go!" Miriam shouted as she ran down the hill.

Jacob's look stopped her as if it had been a slap. But he released Hermann, who slumped, gasping, to the ground. By the time Miriam reached him, he'd caught his breath. Kneeling, he told Jacob, "Next time we fight, you'd better not let me go, because if you do I'll kill you."

JOSEPH: 1947–48

Chapter 20

The week before Founder's Day in 1947, Joseph Gottenberg, Hermann and Miriam's son, left his pickup truck in the Main House parking lot and hurried along the flagstone path to the teepee under the apple tree. As long as he could remember, his Uncle Jacob had lived in a series of bizarre dwellings on this spot. A Navaho hogan. A yurt. A Malayan leaf hut.

One of the earliest dwellings he recalled was a hole in the ground, out of which Jacob sprang like a troll. Joseph had been six. He'd stray down from the yard of the Director's House and wait under the apple tree until Jacob appeared, blinking in the sunlight.

If Joseph was lucky, Jacob would be in a sociable mood and would sit cross-legged in the sun telling stories: fairy tales and myths and legends from all around the world. Sometimes Miriam came down from the house to sit beside them. Occasionally she brought sandwiches and milk or lemonade.

A year earlier, when Joseph was five, he was convinced Jacob was the man in the moon. He thought every night Jacob rose into the sky, losing substance as he drifted up until all that was left was his face, which either covered the disk of the moon like a decal or became the moon, he was never sure which.

And before that, when Joseph was three, he thought Jacob was God, because (and this he figured out many years later) people talked about Jacob and God in the same awed and puzzled tone.

Joseph knew his father disliked Jacob, but even Hermann fed Joseph's confusion about God and Jacob, because he dismissed them both in the same contemptuous way and he objected to Joseph's going to church with Miriam as violently as he objected to Joseph's hanging around with Jacob.

Once—and this was Joseph's first memory of Jacob—Joseph was toddling along the path near what must have been the sweat lodge Joseph later saw in old photographs, when Jacob loomed out of the mouth of the lodge and dragged him into the dark, sweet-smelling interior. Instead of being scared, Joseph felt protected. Perhaps he understood that Jacob was responding to a threat. Joseph had a vague memory of the sky over a field darkening and a rattling noise like thousands of pinwheels spinning.

Years later when Joseph described the memory to Jacob, Jacob stared off at the marble buildings which had been erected in the field where the sky had darkened and said, "Locusts. I never saw anything like it. I don't know if you remember how long we were in that lodge. Hours. I was terrified."

"I wasn't afraid," Joseph said.

"Your mother and father were wild," Jacob said. "They thought you'd been caught out in it."

"That's one time Dad must have been glad you were around," Joseph said.

"Your father thought I was responsible," Jacob said. "Moses bringing a plague on the Egyptians."

Biologically, Hermann was Joseph's father, but in almost every other way he was not. When Joseph got into fights in grade school, he proudly displayed his black eyes to Jacob. During adolescence, he went to Jacob to ask about sex. When Joseph, who had entered high school two years ahead of his class, felt out of place among the older boys and girls, he sought consolation from Jacob. When he announced his intention to study art, Jacob persuaded him to enter medical school. During World War II, when he wanted to join the infantry, Jacob convinced him he'd be of more use as a doctor. After the war, when he wanted to work at St. Elizabeth's Hospital in Washington, D.C., only Jacob could get him to change his mind.

Despite the bond between Joseph and Jacob, when Joseph joined the clinic's staff in the spring of 1946 he didn't side with his uncle. He felt too bound by blood to betray his father; and despite Jacob's influence, Joseph tended to be conservative enough professionally to have reservations about Jacob's increasingly peculiar methods. So, like his mother, Joseph tried to stay neutral. Within months after arriving, he was mediating between his father and his uncle.

For years Hermann had been railroading one expansion plan after another through the board of trustees. A new wing for the back of the Main House; three marble buildings beyond Jacob's apple tree—two dormitories and a new staff office building—which made up the South Quad; a renovation of the old Staff House to make it a guest house for the growing stream of visiting dignitaries; and a model farm, really a farming village, where staff and patients lived together with fewer distinctions between them than in the rest of the clinic. The model farm was on twelve hundred acres half a dozen miles down the Galilee Road from the original site of the clinic, which Hermann had renamed the Old Campus. The year before Joseph started working at the clinic, Hermann had carved out a corner of the model farm's land for the New Campus, which he intended would be a research facility.

Except for the model farm, Jacob had fought each expansion. He was convinced that the more the clinic grew the less effective it would become. He particularly fought the plans for the New Campus. Joseph got them to negotiate. If Jacob would agree to a more modest plan, Hermann would give up his dreams of a sprawling complex of monumental buildings. Just a library, a laboratory, and an auditorium—all of which they needed for the clinic to maintain its credibility in the professional world.

The plan was passed by the board of trustees; the three buildings were built. The last of them, the auditorium, was finished in 1947 just in time for Founder's Day. Every year, under Hermann's direction, Founder's Day had become more and more spectacular. In 1947, with the dedication of the New Campus, it would be the most magnificent yet. The President of the United States sent a congratulatory telegram, and there was even a rumor—which turned out to be false—that Jung would show up. The highlight of the weekend would be a fund-raising dinner to honor Abraham.

Abraham, now eighty-eight, was frail. His face was cadaverous. His chest was sunken. His legs were weak. But he was still lucid. Ever since Rosa had died, a decade and a half earlier, he had withdrawn to his tower room to read and write, producing a book a year. His style was folksy, so his books were popular with the general public, which sought in them what one reviewer called "a commonsensical approach to psychoanalysis"—a description Abraham loathed.

The books piling up in his room made a precarious wall between him and the door. By 1940 there were so many copies of his books and magazine articles spread across the floor that there was little room to move, only narrow paths that led from the door to the bed and from the bed to the desk and from the desk to the rocker by the window —from which Abraham gazed at the clinic, his creation, below.

Although he rarely appeared in public, he agreed to give a speech at the Founder's Day dinner. Hermann spent days going over the program.

"I want you to introduce the Director," he told Jacob.

"If you stop interfering with my show," Jacob said.

To inaugurate the auditorium, Jacob wanted to put on a production of *A Midsummer Night's Dream,* which his patients had been rehearsing. He'd been having good results with what he dubbed "theatrical therapy." His patients had performed scenes from *Othello, King Lear, Richard III,* and *Coriolanus* for the clinic, but this was their first full-length production.

Hermann's opposition to the performance had been tactical—he wanted a bargaining chip to use with his brother—just as Jacob's threat to boycott the dinner was tactical. Since Hermann didn't care if the play was performed and Jacob would never miss the dinner, their quarrel was unnecessary. But it gave each a chance to feel he was imposing his will on the other.

On Saturday night, Jacob would introduce Abraham, and after the banquet, *A Midsummer Night's Dream* would inaugurate the auditorium.

At the end of the flagstone path, Joseph stopped. Jacob, sitting cross-legged in front of the teepee, was watching Oberon and Puck rehearse a scene.

Joseph squatted beside his uncle.

"It's not the Old Vic," Jacob said, "but they've all learned their lines."

"Did you hear about Dad's surprise?" Joseph asked.

"Oh, yes," Jacob said. "Keeps busy, my brother, doesn't he?"

Despite his promise, Hermann had not satisfied himself with three new buildings. He secretly had negotiated with Leverett Stratton, a New York real estate developer whose wife had spent two years at the clinic. She'd been hollowed out by cancer, turned into a human drum, so even the slightest emotional blow was amplified. Miriam had gained her trust and midwifed her death. Stratton was grateful enough for his wife's relatively peaceful end that he wanted to endow the clinic with a building fund, enough to complete the New Campus: three laboratories, staff quarters, a gymnasium, and a dining hall. Hermann had announced the scheme that morning. Good timing. The trustees, gathered in Galilee for the celebration, could be stampeded. It would be hard to turn down so large an endowment. A meeting of the board had been called for the day after the dinner.

Joseph lay back on the grass and stared up at the branches of the apple tree. Long ago, on Hermann's orders it had been stripped of Jacob's trinkets. But when Joseph had been a child, he'd thought it a great honor to help hang the flashy junk, more special than decorating a Christmas tree.

"Do you ever regret staying at the clinic?" Joseph asked.

"Do you?" Jacob asked back.

Jacob looked down at his nephew, whose face always seemed so drawn, so tense with expectation, as though the future were a debilitating disease. He wanted to embrace Joseph, to comfort him as one would a child; and he wondered if Hermann could possibly love Joseph more than he did.

"How are you going to vote?" Jacob asked.

"We need the buildings," Joseph said.

* * *

The star of Jacob's production of *A Midsummer Night's Dream* was a patient named Clark Daly, a movie actor who in fact had given Jacob the inspiration for the theatrical therapy when he arrived at the clinic. Daly had started his movie career playing clean-cut sidekicks and younger brothers. He was not handsome in his youth, but he had regular features and a dazzling smile. As he grew older, different parts of his face seemed to age at different rates, which gave him a twisted, almost ugly look. It also made him unique. No longer could he be confused with the dozens of other actors who specialized in clean-cut sidekicks and younger brothers.

In 1932, Warner Brothers, not knowing what to do with him, cast him as Friar Ambrosio in *The Monk,* a wonderful part: a pious man destroyed by lust, who (and this, of course, was never made explicit) murders his mother, rapes and kills his sister, and in the end sells his soul to the devil. Even in the last scene, lit from beneath so his grin was ghoulish and his eyebrows seemed peaked as pine trees, he maintained a dignity that women in the audience found erotic. He became a star, the sinister mirror image of his earlier clean-cut parts.

There followed a series of roles, each more villainously romantic than the last: *The Bottle Imp, The Coffin Lid, The Lord of Babylon, The Last Man, The Blind Spot.* Because most of the atrocities were softened by censors into mere hints of naughtiness, his evil always seemed innocent, more a matter of style than substance. A depraved glitter to the eye. A lascivious smile.

His masterpiece was *Gilles de Rais,* which he played with vaudevillian flourish, as though the monster were not a bloodthirsty pervert, but a baggy-trousered top banana. The public was as outraged as if he'd committed sacrilege, defiling the purity of his evil by making fun of it. The movie bombed.

He returned to his formula for his next three films, in

which he played various dissolute dukes. Although they did well, his reputation had been fatally infected by his best role. After *Gilles de Rais*, all his villains seemed to be repressing not smoldering sadistic sexuality but slapstick.

The year before the studio sent him to the clinic, he'd filmed the second best role of his career, *Benvenuto Cellini*. He had the perfect pompous swagger for the part. He was the ideal mix of charlatan and hero.

But he began to confuse himself with his roles. He designed a coat of arms with a scull, raven, and quill, and built a castle with trapdoors, secret passageways, and a dungeon in which—it was rumored—unsavory parties took place. When these rumors threatened to spark a general censorship campaign against Hollywood, the studio insisted that Daly "take a rest cure" at the clinic.

Whenever he met someone new, Daly repeated the story of how he'd been railroaded. His latest victim was Lee Stratton, the daughter of the man who was endowing Hermann's building fund. After breakfasting in the Guest House, she'd wandered down toward the Main House, where she recognized Daly. When she asked him for his autograph, he launched into his tale.

Until then it hadn't occurred to her that he might be a patient. He was dressed in ordinary clothes. But while he raved she began backing away. Daly followed until he'd trapped her against the Main House wall. He was harmless, just overly enthusiastic.

"Now, imagine the scene," he said. "We're sitting—these producers, these moguls of moguls, and me—on a lawn as green as, well, what you think grass *should* look like. I mean, it was perfect. And over there, way across the fucking lawn, were these peons painting with green paint—can you believe it—the brown spots where the grass had died, probably piddled on by one of those Russian dogs that were lying around. You know those dogs. They look like they came off someone's bookplate.

I mean everything was so perfect it was unreal. Unreal. And they're saying to me *I've* lost touch and have to go off to someplace 'peaceful'—no, wait a minute—'tranquil,' that's it, 'tranquil surroundings'—to recover from my nervous breakdown."

" 'But I'm not suffering from any nervous breakdown,' I say.

" 'What about your—ah—escapades?' they say.

"So discreet. Except these are guys who have women on staff just to shove salamis up their asses while singing the *Sh'ma*."

Lee hit Daly on the chest, face, shoulder. Dumbstruck, Daly stepped back and back. Lee followed him, flailing. Joseph, having just left his uncle, noticed the scene. Coming up behind Lee, he hugged her, pinning her arms. Thinking she was being attacked by another patient, Lee stamped on Joseph's instep with the heel of her shoe.

"Son of a bitch," Joseph said, releasing her.

Spinning around, she slugged Joseph in the ear. Joseph cried out and held the side of his head. Lee recognized him; they'd been introduced when she first arrived.

"I didn't know—" she started. "Why'd you grab me?"

Joseph, whose ear was still ringing, said, "You can't go around beating up our patients. Or our staff."

"I was just telling her—" Daly said.

"I know what you were telling her," Joseph interrupted.

"Your ear's all red," she said. "I'm sorry."

She kissed Joseph's ear and headed back up the hill to the Guest House.

Joseph was more startled by the kiss than by the attack. He turned to Daly, who said, "I don't know why she kissed *you*. She hit me harder."

At the last minute, Abraham, too weak to attend, canceled his appearance at the dinner. Hermann refused to change the seating arrangements, so everyone honored Abraham's empty chair.

After the ceremony, the auditorium lights dimmed and the stage lights came on.

The curtains opened on a stylized Athens filled with plaster statues—which Jacob, indulging in a private joke, had chosen for their resemblance to people he knew. A Zeus with a star burst of hair, a thundercloud beard, and a bison's face, which looked like Abraham in his prime. Ares, arm raised and index finger extended, his tunic so tightly fitted that the decorative figures on it looked carved into the flesh of his chest—Hermann as a young man. Dionysus with impish, almost Oriental eyes and a beard like beer foam—Jacob as he looked now. But with all the statues onstage, the scene looked less like a city than a graveyard.

The production was no better than most amateur efforts; and despite the cast of patients, it was no worse. At the end, the audience applauded wildly, as though congratulating not just the actors but themselves for sitting through it. But the houselights did not go on immediately. The actors, maintaining their roles as fairies and enchanted mortals, drifted off the stage and through the audience, singing the song from Act II.

> Over hill, over dale,
>   Through bush, through briar,
> Over park, over pale,
>   Through flood, through fire,
> I do wander everywhere . . .

Jacob had intended this mingling of actors and audience to be a bridge between the play and reality and between the patients and visitors. He assumed people would be amused, conversations would start, the patients families would meet each other.

But although no one in the cast was a serious case, the audience grew uneasy. They would have been disturbed even if the actors were certifiably sane. They felt invaded, their immunity as observers violated.

Daly was an acute enough observer to note the reaction, and had enough of the patients' contempt for what he called *civilians* (translating the actors' term for nonactors into an inmates' term for noninmates) to enjoy the visitors' discomfort. Wearing the ass's head from his costume, he wandered from table to table and harangued the guests, dipping his fingers into their glasses and flicking water at them.

"'Women,' my father used to say," said Daly, "'are nothing more than breasts, bellies, and backsides. The three B's,' he called them. He was a horny old man. A carpenter. Right out of some locker-room joke. He'd get brought in on nothing jobs by bored housewives. 'Please, Mr. Lockley'—that's my family's real name—'could you plane this rough spot, sandpaper that bump, file my door down . . .' Lots of friction. He knew what he was talking about, all right. 'Women,' he said, 'are like lice. If you're not careful, you can spend your whole life scratching.'"

When Jacob, Hermann, Joseph, and a dozen of the other staff members jumped up to stop him, Daly bolted across the room and out a door into the night.

About half of the other actors followed him, some out of confusion and some out of rebellious high spirits.

The weather was mild. The moon was rising. Bottom, Oberon, Puck, Titania, Theseus, Snug, Snout, Starveling, Cobweb, Moth, and Mustardseed—all in costume: togas and spangled gauze—wandered back toward the Old Campus in shifting groups of twos and threes, startling the people who lived in the recently built houses along the roadside, who, nervous about settling so close to the clinic, had always expected something like this to happen. All along the way, lights went on in bedrooms as neighbors who were awake called neighbors who were asleep to warn them the lunatics were loose.

Most of the actors were subdued after their breakout, but Daly shouted at the top of his lungs speeches from his more bloodthirsty movies.

"Knock it off," said the actor who played Starveling, a premed student who had suffered a nervous breakdown during exams at Columbia.

A car passing in the opposite direction flashed its headlights at them. They blinked and hitched up their dragging costumes. They could have been a band of aging trick-or-treaters out on Halloween.

When Joseph's truck passed and parked on the side of the road, most of them stopped. Two staff cars, each carrying half a dozen orderlies, pulled up behind, boxing them in.

Kriger got out of the first car.

"It's okay," Joseph said.

Kriger looked dubious.

"Everything's under control," Joseph said.

He wanted to minimize the trouble to protect Jacob, who he knew would be blamed.

Kriger climbed back behind his steering wheel. Both cars made U-turns and headed down the road toward the auditorium, where the celebration was still going on.

Leaving his motor running, Joseph stood by the back of his truck and told the patients, "Get in."

They hoisted themselves onto the flatbed of the truck like infantrymen exhausted from a day's hike. They sat, knees raised, in a semicircle along the wooden side-slats.

Only Starveling and Daly did not climb in.

"I want to walk home," Starveling said.

"I can't let you," Joseph said.

"You think I'm going to break into one of these sweet

homes and rape and murder an innocent family," Starveling said.

"No such thing as an innocent family," Daly said.

"You get in too, Daly," Joseph said.

"You don't know what dreadful things go on in those houses," Daly said to Starveling. "Wife beating, child abuse, incest . . ."

"Let's go," Joseph said.

"Ordinary people," Daly said. "Drunks, degenerates, fornicators, misers, gluttons, sensualists, brutes, lechers, liars, hotheads, braggarts, toadies, hangers-on, stuffed shirts, prudes and prigs, cowards, flatterers, sneaks, humbugs, fools—"

"Let's go," Joseph repeated.

"All of them envious, greedy, self-centered, proud, petty, sullen, peevish, petulant, belligerent, ungrateful, unforgiving, unremorseful, cynical, cruel, ruthless, spiteful, malicious, mean, coldhearted, callous, rude, dissembling, insolent—"

"In the truck," Joseph said.

"Vain," Daly said, "self-satisfied, servile, shameless, condescending, pompous, vindictive, deceitful, unctuous, treacherous, spineless, fickle, conceited, lazy—"

"Daly," Joseph said, "what's the matter with you?"

"What's the matter with me?" Daly asked. "The same thing that's the matter with him." He pointed at Starveling. "With them." He pointed at the others in the back of the truck. "With you. And them." He waved to include the houses and the people whose heads stuck out of windows. "Everything's the matter."

"Come on." Joseph put his arm around Daly's shoulders.

"You pretend to be sympathetic almost as well as I pretend to be crazy," Daly said.

"Only make-believe?" Joseph asked.

Daly shrugged. "I might as well give them their money's worth," he said, gesturing toward the faces in the windows of the nearby houses. Raising his hands over his head like paws, he gave his famous insane movie laugh.

"That ought to hold them," he said. He climbed into the cab of the truck through the passenger door.

"Okay," Joseph said to Starveling, who heaved himself onto the bed of the truck just as the truck started moving.

"Hey!" Joseph called, running after the accelerating truck.

Daly, behind the steering wheel, leaned out the window and called, "See you at the clinic, Doc."

The truck disappeared around a bend in the road.

Joseph wanted to call the clinic, but no one in any of the houses along the road would let him in. Even after Joseph assured them that he was not a patient but a doctor, they kept their doors bolted.

"I don't care what you are," said one man, who flipped up the hinged flap of his letter slot and talked through the narrow opening. "I've got a shotgun in here, and if any of you people try to break in, I'll blast you to kingdom come."

"Why would I break in?" Joseph asked.

"Get!" the man shouted.

The letter-slot flap snapped back into place.

The house was new. Stacks of lumber, giving off sweet whiffs of cut wood, lay next to a shallow hole dug for the foundation of a garage. A cat or large rat slithered underneath an overturned wheelbarrow. To vent his anger, Joseph picked up two fragments of brick. He tossed one at the wheelbarrow. It clanged against the metal and sent the creature scurrying. He threw the other. He did not even aim, never expected it to hit; but it did, and killed the animal, a cat. When Joseph picked up the warm body, blood spilled over his chest, forearms, and hands. He took the corpse to the house.

"I've killed your cat!" he shouted.

The light upstairs went off. The house was dark.

"I've killed your cat!" Joseph shouted again.

The man yelled, "Get! Or, by Christ, I'll blast you!"

Joseph laid the cat's body on the back porch and hurried away.

He took a shortcut to the clinic through some fields, realizing halfway there—as he saw the headlights of the cars returning from the auditorium—that he should have stuck to the road. He hoped Daly had driven right back to the Old Campus—which he had. Joseph found the truck abandoned halfway between the Director's House and the Guest House. He correctly assumed that Daly and the other patients had returned to their dormitory rooms. Although a few cars turned down the clinic road toward the parking lot and people strolled along various paths, the Old Campus was quiet. The crisis was over.

Joseph tried to start the truck, but the motor just made a hammering noise. Probably that was why Daly had abandoned it. Joseph tried to start it again; the motor again hammered, each metallic thunk reminding Joseph of the sound of the brick against the bottom of the wheelbarrow.

When he turned off the motor, he heard a woman's voice calling, "What's that racket?"

"Sorry!" Joseph shouted, as he scanned the clinic grounds.

"Need help?" the voice asked.

Joseph walked a few steps from the car to get a clearer look down the hill.

"Up here," the voice said.

Peering from a second-floor window over the porch roof of the Guest House was Stratton's daughter, Lee. She was framed in the window, back-lit by the light in her room so her body showed up as a silhouette inside her nightgown. Joseph felt a thunk in his chest, as if Lee had just lobbed something as hard as a brick against his heart.

"Wait a minute," he called.

He climbed the iron trellis through the ivy, scrambled diagonally across the slippery slate roof, and perched outside her window.

"What are you doing?" she said.

"I had to talk to you," Joseph said.

"I could have come down," she said.

They grinned at each other.

"What if someone sees you?" she asked.

"I'd be in big trouble," he said.

Suddenly, she made a face. It was a startling, childish thing to do. Joseph thought she was trying to be as spontaneous and antic as he'd been in climbing the trellis, and felt embarrassed for her, because it seemed like such a premeditated, insincere effort. To put her at her ease, he made a face back.

But he was wrong. Her grimace was sincere. She'd just noticed the blood all over him.

"What have you done?" she asked. "You've murdered someone."

Joseph glanced down at his shirt.

"I killed a cat," he said.

"Oh my God," she said, backing away.

"An accident," he said.

When he finished explaining, she said, "How awful for you."

For a moment, both were silent.

"An angel passed," she said.

"What did you think of the play?" Joseph asked, desperate for something to say.

"You didn't come all the way up here to ask that," she said.

"I don't know why I came up here," he said. "It's been a strange night."

"You'd better go," she said.

Joseph slid back along the roof and climbed down the trellis. Before going into the Director's House, he looked at the Guest House. Lee's light was off, but he was sure she was still watching him.

Hermann stayed up all night to deal with the police and various public officials from Galilee who responded to the dozens of hysterical calls from the people who lived near the clinic. At six-thirty, just when he thought everything had settled down, he got another call from the police, who said one of the patients had killed a cat and maliciously left it on the owner's porch.

Hermann exploded. It was all Jacob's fault: if he hadn't insisted on performing the play, the patients wouldn't have run wild. Something had to be done.

Twice during the night Miriam had prevented Hermann from waking Abraham to either demand Jacob's resignation or submit his own. Now Miriam couldn't stop him.

In the kitchen, Hermann threw together a breakfast tray for his father. He stormed up to the tower room, the teacup rattling in its saucer.

Abraham lay in bed, his body making skeletal bumps and ridges under a sheet. He opened his eyes as Hermann entered.

"This time Jacob's gone too far," Hermann said.

Abraham, who was not as deaf as he pretended, used the deafness to ignore Hermann.

"Help me sit up," he said. Age had given him an old woman's voice.

Hermann clapped the tray on a bedside table. He wormed his arm under his father's bony back and held him up while with his other hand he plumped pillows.

"Last night—" Hermann began.

"Hand me my tray," Abraham said.

Hermann swung down the tray legs and fitted the tray over his father's shrunken lap.

Abraham licked his lips. His tongue was yellow.

"After the performance—" Hermann began.

"Could you put some jam on my toast?" Abraham asked.

"Pa," Hermann said, "listen to me."

He smeared jam on the toast as he recited the previous night's events, ending with a demand that Abraham at least attend the board meeting and disavow Jacob's recklessness to make sure Stratton did not withdraw his endowment.

"Look at me," Abraham said. "How can I go?"

Hermann, uncomfortable at his father's calm and his own hysteria, busied himself with preparing another piece of toast.

"At least write a letter I can read to the board," he said.

"On one condition," Abraham said.

Hermann looked up. He hadn't expected his father to agree.

"You let Jacob continue his work here," Abraham said. "Without interference."

"Yes," Hermann said.

"As long as he lives," Abraham said.

"I will," Hermann said. With a napkin, he dabbed at some jam on his father's chin.

"Get me paper and pen," Abraham said. "Clear the tray."

Laboriously, Abraham wrote two pages in handwriting which had gotten large and shaky as a child's first efforts. He folded the paper, creasing it with his wrist.

"Now," he said, "take it and go."

Smiling, Hermann started to leave.

"Oh, yes," Abraham added. "Tell your brother I want to talk to him at four."

"The board meets at four," Hermann said.

"I know," Abraham said.

Jacob arrived at three forty-five, hoping to get through the interview in time for the board meeting. Abraham propped against the headboard of the bed, did not move as Jacob entered.

Thinking about the board meeting, Jacob said, "If you're tired I can come back later."

"Give me your hand," Abraham said.

Jacob held out his hand, which his father's clawlike fingers grasped—so tightly Jacob winced. He was surprised his father still had such strength.

"I wrote a letter for Hermann to read at the board meeting," Abraham said. "It condemns in particular what I gather happened last night and in general your unorthodox procedures."

Jacob started to pull his hand away, but Abraham held it fast.

"Furthermore," Abraham continued, "I'm casting my vote for Hermann's building program. And—it's time I finally made a choice—I recommended Hermann be made director of the clinic. Now stop squirming. He's got a better head for business than you do, and the clinic's become big business."

For the first time in a quarter of a century, Jacob felt like crying.

"I want you to make me a promise," Abraham said. "I want you to promise to stay at the clinic."

"With Hermann in control?" Jacob asked.

"Promise," Abraham said.

"No," Jacob said.

"Do I have to threaten you?" Abraham said.

"You wouldn't let me leave when I was a kid," Jacob said, "and you won't let me leave now."

"Where would you go?" Abraham said. "This is home."

"Hermann's home," Jacob said.

"He'll leave you alone," Abraham said. "I promise."

"You're right," Jacob said. "Where would I go?"

Abraham struggled to sit up. When Jacob reached out to help him, he said, "No, no, I'm all right. I suppose it's not just old-fashioned but antique for a father to bestow a deathbed blessing. But, Jacob, are you listening? You have my blessing."

"Deathbed?" Jacob said. "Oh, Pa—"

"Pay attention," Abraham said. "This is supposed to be a solemn moment."

He let go of Jacob's hand. Around the wrist were white marks where Abraham had dug his nails in.

"Go," Abraham said. "With my blessing."

At the door, Jacob turned, ready to argue with his father —about his decision to make Hermann director of the clinic, about his demand that Jacob stay on. But Abraham's pupils were rolled up, as though he were astonished by something he'd just seen on the ceiling. Having given the clinic to one son and his blessing to the other, Abraham had died.

Chapter 21

Hermann didn't follow Abraham's wishes. Although he left Jacob alone professionally, he forbade him to camp on the clinic's grounds—because he said he was worried about Jacob's health—and he cut down Jacob's apple tree—which he claimed was diseased. He even uprooted the tree's stump and reseeded the whole area with a new kind of grass which had been developed for golf courses.

Joseph, furious at his father, decided to quit.

Three months after Abraham's death, he woke at dawn; packed the ancient gladstone bag he'd found in the attic of the Director's House; furtively washed, shaved, and dressed; and climbed the stairs to the tower room, which Hermann, now director of the clinic, had claimed as his new office. All of Abraham's clutter had been catalogued and carted off to the old library in the Main House, where it was added to the collection of memorabilia.

The room now had Hermann's look. On the floor lay an

Oriental rug. Next to a new couch was a large console radio with shortwave as well as broadcast bands. Scholarly journals were fanned out on the low glass-topped coffee table. One free wall was ornamented with Hermann's diplomas and honorary citations; the other with an original Dürer etching of a hawk and a snake. Built-in bookcases covered the other two walls. The shelves surrounded windows, which offered views through the massed books of (in one direction) the South Quad and (in the other direction) the spot where Jacob used to camp.

Abraham's old desk remained, but its polished top was empty except for a pen stand, a diary with a black leather cover stamped in gold leaf, and a block of wood the size of a fist—all that was left of the apple tree. On one smoothed side was a brass plaque, which said: FROM THE ORIGINAL SITE OF THE GOTTENBERG CLINIC. As much as the tree had infuriated him when Jacob was bedecking it, now that it was gone Hermann had appropriated it as part of the clinic's history.

Joseph slipped his letter of resignation under the edge of the diary. It was a simple formal statement. He gave no reason for quitting.

He picked up the block of wood and rubbed his thumb back and forth over the raised letters on the plaque. Then he stuck the wood in his pocket and left the tower.

All Joseph took to New York City was the block of wood, a few changes of clothes, his shaving kit, and a journal. During his first month, Joseph chastely cased the sexual life of the city, visiting the waterfront, where women lifted their dresses for their customers in doorways or alleys; whorehouses in Lower East Side tenements, where beds, six or seven to a room, were separated by filthy curtains; private apartments in the Village; hotels in the West Thirties; ballrooms on Seventh Avenue where men ground against the taxi dancers who gazed vacantly over their shoulders and popped their gum; elegant bordellos off Fifth Avenue in the mid-Fifties; back-room clubs along Jungle Alley in Harlem; rent parties, drags, sporting cafés . . .

He gradually became a recognized figure of fun: the lanky man in the English drape suit who paid to talk and take notes. Once it was clear he was not a cop or crusader, whores vied to be with him, since all they had to do for their money was answer questions. He was most interested in what customers said they wanted and how they reacted when the whores fulfilled their desires. At first some of the women made up stories, but he was a careful cross-examiner and always tripped them up in their lies.

One whore named Kate interrupted a session to ask, "What are you after?"

Joseph was primly propped on the edge of her bed, note pad and pen in hand. Kate, sitting cross-legged on her pillow like a pasha, was naked except for a G-string. Her breasts were tubular. Her belly was a washboard of lateral creases. The pubic hairs, curling from under her G-string were as precise as architectural details. She was not pretty: her face was too broad, her complexion grainy. But she had a knack for concentration, which in her work was happily mistaken for passion.

This was the third time Joseph had visited her. He kept coming back because her questions—like the one she'd just asked—led him to believe she was interested in his work. In fact, she was just staving off boredom.

"I'm trying to understand what people do when they reach their limits," Joseph said.

"You mean the freaks?" she asked.

"Everyone has limits," Joseph said.

"Normals too?" she asked.

"Have you ever met a normal?" Joseph asked.

"What's a normal?" she said, suddenly cagey, as though she feared he was asking a trick question.

"I don't know," Joseph said. "In your business, what's a normal?"

"If they're normal," she said, "they don't come here."

"Even me, you're thinking," Joseph said.

"Yeah, well, you're an oddball all right," she said.

She stretched out her legs and massaged a cramp in her left thigh. The crotch of her G-string pressed into her cunt, separating the lips, two rolls of flesh brown as cattails.

"So in your business," she asked, "what's a normal? Why are you smiling?"

"If they're normal," he said, "they don't come to me either."

"Yeah," she said. "So where do they all hang out, the normals?"

Joseph tapped his forehead. "We pretend they exist to give us hope," he said.

She got up on her hands and knees and crawled down the bed toward Joseph, her breasts swinging like censers.

"So what do people do when they reach their limits?" she asked.

"Different people do different things," Joseph said.

"And you can learn that from asking all these questions?" she asked.

Joseph looked down at his notebook for an answer.

"Seems to me," she said, "you're trying to find out what an orange tastes like by asking, when all you have to do is take a bite."

"That wouldn't be scientific," he said.

"Well," she said, "do you want to be scientific or do you want to know?"

That night, Joseph collared the hood who ran the place,

a Jew named Loone, who dressed like a banker and talked like a tout.

"How much to set me up in a room with a peephole so I can watch the action?" Joseph asked.

"What is this?" Loone asked. "Blackmail?"

"Science," Joseph said.

He explained as much as he could. Loone, no dope, said, "You won't get somebodies to watch—just in case your notes may happen to fall into the hands of anybody they shouldn't. You'll get just nobodies. Nothings. We call 'em our ghosts."

They drilled a hole through a wall.

Believing Kate would be able to talk about her impressions more clearly than the others, Joseph asked Loone to put her in the room he was watching. Kate demanded money. Loone shrugged. That wasn't his business. Joseph had already paid him. If Kate wanted to make a separate arrangement . . .

Joseph offered to double whatever Kate made while he watched.

Kate sashayed into the room. Joseph went next door to his peephole post.

She lay down on the mattress and propped one heel against the metal rail at the foot of the bed and the other on a chair, so she was spread for Joseph to see.

He turned away from the peephole.

"Let me know when you go to work," he called.

She laughed.

Her first customer that night was a young man, mid-twenties, well dressed in a conservative gray suit, college-educated from his accent. He could have been Joseph.

After the preliminaries—Kate taking his money, washing him, milking him to make sure he wasn't diseased—he told Kate to squat on the bed as he sat on a chair and masturbated.

"Do you want me to do anything else?" Kate asked.

"Turn around," he said in a strangled voice.

She duck-walked around until she was facing away from him.

"Anything else?" she asked.

He stretched out his legs and, after a moment more, grunted.

"You through?" Kate asked. She tossed him a towel.

Joseph stuck his notebook under an arm and left the room. Downstairs, he told Loone, "I'll be back tomorrow night."

For the next three weeks, every night Joseph perched on a high stool like a clerk in a Dickens novel, his face pressed so hard against the peephole that when he pulled away he had a welt that ringed his eye like a monocle. On his lap lay his notebook, big as a cathedral's Bible. The pages were vertically ruled. In the first column he jotted brief descriptions of what he saw; in the second, snatches of dialogue; in the third, quick sketches; in the fourth, fragments of instant analysis. Every night after going home, he used the notes to write detailed reports, which he cross-referenced in the back of the book by desires and perversions.

During the day, after reading in the public library, he hung out at burlesque shows, studying the faces of the men straining forward, flushed and intent as though transfigured by worship, as though pornography were all that remained of the rites of an ancient religion.

"Sometimes it seems so innocent," he wrote home, "like what kids do in secret: you show me yours and I'll show you mine. And other times, not foul, but alien, like something from another planet."

Hermann ignored all Joseph's thoughts on his work in New York.

Miriam expressed cautious interest and gave practical advice. "Don't just catalogue," she wrote, and she sent him her volumes of Stekel.

Jacob was fascinated. But like Kate he wondered if Joseph's approach would work.

"Can you understand obsession from the outside?" he wrote. "Can you understand any experience from the outside? That's always been my argument with your father."

As Joseph's notes piled up—in less than a month he'd filled four 300-page notebooks—his curiosity led him to finer and finer distinctions, discriminations the whores found silly: the differences between men who wanted to be fellated by women with thick lips or thin, buck teeth or bad teeth; who were aroused by women with certain haircuts, moles or no moles, large nipples or small—all the erotic subtleties that were so important to the johns, qualities or actions the men would insist on every time they visited, as though these details were clues to something that kept eluding them, as though by repeating the same experience over and over they finally would stumble on the secret meaning of that specific coincidence of person, place, and act. Joseph felt like an anthropologist who'd discovered a culture in which each individual had developed a unique and complex ritual for teasing out the mystery of life.

One afternoon in early August, Joseph had just left the twilight of a burlesque show and was crossing Sixth Avenue when he noticed a sign fixed to a chain-link fence around an excavation. In the middle of the sign, crowded on top and bottom by information about the project under way, was: STRATTON CONSTRUCTION CO.

Watching the yellow bulldozers crawling around in the

pit, Joseph realized the real reason he'd come to New York was to be near Lee. Ducking into a nearby hotel, he riffled through a telephone book and found Stratton's name. He jotted the information down on the inside cover of his sex research notebook and started the trek to Park Avenue and Ninetieth Street, where the Strattons lived. He wanted a chance to think.

On East Eighty-sixth Street, Joseph stopped at a lunch counter. A small fan stirred the strips of flypaper, which were encrusted with dead insects. Behind the counter, tacked to the wall, was a calendar with a picture of a woman in a farm girl's flouncy dress bending over to collect eggs and showing impossibly pink, plump thighs. At the back of the long room was a pinball machine with a display of a cartoon glamor girl, constellations of sequins placed over breasts and crotch. The cartoon was so broad, so unrealistic it seemed ridiculous to invest it with such coy sexuality. But as Joseph sipped his soda, he surprised himself by becoming aroused as his imagination filled in the hidden features, even though, oddly, the features he imagined were no less cartoony than the rest of the figure.

When he rang Stratton's bell, he was still aroused. The memory of the cartoon breasts and crotch that he himself had dreamed into existence tugged at his attention.

A maid in a starched bib apron opened the door. She took his hat and left him in the living room.

Lee appeared in a Japanese-style gown. A dragon the green of a blowfly coiled from her hem up one leg and around her waist, spreading its claws over her breasts. Her hair, very short, was the blue-black of oil. He didn't remember her having short hair. Her lipstick was very red. Had she worn lipstick at the clinic? Her chin was sharper than he recalled, her mouth smaller. Her eyebrows, plucked and penciled, swept up her forehead like antennae.

But once they sat on a living room couch, she as attentive as a schoolgirl, everything that had seemed sinister—the dragon design, the too red lips—lost its threat. Joseph couldn't understand what had made everything so menacing.

They went to a restaurant in Yorkville, where they ordered strudel and coffee, which they ignored. They talked, both of them as intent as the men Joseph had seen in the burlesque houses. The subjects were inconsequential, but never before had Joseph experienced such mutual understanding. Everything they said seemed to be a code both knew by heart.

As they walked back to Lee's apartment, she took from her purse a packet of the same lemon lozenges that Kate sucked on after fellating her customers. Joseph realized he hadn't mentioned what he was doing in New York and that he didn't want to tell her—not because he wanted to protect her from something unsavory. His feelings about the world he was studying were more complex than that. Maybe, he thought, he was protecting her from complexity.

When they kissed under the awning of her building, he tasted the lemon flavor of her lozenge.

That night, while waiting for a customer, Kate, as usual, dragged her chair next to the peephole, so she and Joseph could converse like prisoners through the small opening.

"Why don't you come in here tonight?" she asked.

"Why do you want me to?" Joseph asked back.

"Why don't you want to?" she asked.

"I couldn't take notes," he said.

"I'll remember everything and remind you afterwards," she said. "I'll draw you pictures."

"What if I said I'd like to?" he asked.

"I'd say you're telling the truth," she said.

She bent down to peer through the hole. All she saw was a patch of cloth: Joseph's jacket.

"But you won't," she said.

"No," he said. "I won't."

She put a finger up her cunt and poked it through the hole.

"Sniff," she said.

"Don't be ridiculous," Joseph said.

She pulled back her finger.

"You son of a bitch," she said. "I'm offering you a free sample. Hey, talking to you like this, I feel I'm in confession."

"What could you have left to confess?" Joseph asked. "I've seen everything."

"Everyone has secrets," she said.

Secrets. Joseph felt he wasn't discovering secrets so much as tuning in on a parallel world. This left him with the same frustrations he used to have when he fiddled with the cat whisker of his crystal set, trying to discover the spot on the crystal which would bring in the signal strongest. Sometimes as he watched Kate and her customers, he'd be overwhelmed by indifference. He felt like a man on a train watching fields and towns flash past. There was life out there, but it had nothing to do with him. Other times he felt on the verge of understanding something compelling and profound about human nature —something clear, but so strange he couldn't find words to express it. It was like seeing a common object photographed in such an odd way that it was impossible to tell what it was.

He began wondering what caused the difference in his feelings. Was it something occurring between Kate and her customers? Their involvement in each other or their estrangement? How aroused the john was, how accommodating Kate was? How bizarre the request, how interesting the reaction to having the request met?

Tutored by Joseph, Kate would cozy up to a customer and ask, "Now what would you really like to do? Something you never done before and always wanted?"

Oral sex; anal sex; masturbation; exhibitionism; voyeurism; sadism; masochism; flagellation; transvestism; urolagnia; coprophilia; bondage and discipline, bondage by itself, the idea but not the act of bondage; hand, breast, buttock, stocking, panty, shoe, foot fetishism—but not just foot fetishism: some men were specialists, aroused by specific parts of the foot, the arch, the heel, the toe, or even by a particular toe, the big toe on the left foot or the middle toe on the right, or even parts of the particular toe, the tip, the pad, the nail . . . Kate's customers were scientists, breaking the erotic down into finer and finer categories, Linnaeuses of lust.

Not just scientists, but artists, too—because, like artists, they were perfectionists, masters of nuance. Everything had to be just right for them to be satisfied. They knew how to select and frame fragments of life, which were charged with meaning by the very act of being isolated. Arousal, as Joseph learned, was merely a matter of attention. Anything could be sexualized, not just orifices but surfaces, not just things that touched the body but things that touched things that touched the body. Sympathetic magic. Kate's customers were, therefore, not just scientists and artists but also magicians, guiding power from its source into more and more removed objects, power becoming attenuated with every displacement and needing to be concentrated in smaller and smaller areas to produce its effects.

And Kate was a demon conjured up to create realities. She produced corsets for corset fetishes, other women for lesbian shows, men for homosexuals, dogs for bestiality.

She was costumer, prop mistress, and ringmaster for a sexual circus; the room was at the same time big top, menagerie, and sideshow. Kate had dildos, masks, whips, restraints, all the armamentarium of perversion. A good scout, she was prepared for every contingency.

Some men, having admitted and then experienced their previously unspoken desires, left invigorated; others left broken on the wheel of their own imagination. It did not matter whether their desires were extreme or innocent. What mattered was what their particular limits were.

A man who pricked the tips of Kate's fingers and had her masturbate him with her bloody hand said afterward, "I never even knew I wanted to do that."

As he sat on the edge of the bed, half dressed, amazed by his own perversion, he seemed to become more and more vivid, as though he were (as Loone had jokingly called Kate's customers) a ghost—a ghost that was materializing as Joseph watched.

Another of Kate's johns, a man who simply wanted to talk dirty as he fucked her, could barely dress himself afterward, he was so shaken by violating his limits. When Kate asked him if he was all right, she (and Joseph behind the peephole) could hardly hear his answer, his voice had faded so from humiliation and guilt. He too seemed a ghost, but one that was dematerializing.

More and more Joseph thought of the customers as ghosts, spirits in the process of vanishing or becoming increasingly real, soon to be reborn into the world. Kate was the goddess presiding over their extinction or rebirth.

The fluctuating interest with which Joseph watched, he realized, was a product of what went on not in Kate's room but inside himself, as though Joseph as much as Kate's customers were a ghost, but a ghost whose destiny was undecided, sometimes taking on and sometimes losing substance, the world around him becoming vivid or dim depending on how real he was, depending on how close he approached or how far he withdrew from his own limit. And his limit was the barrier that separated the observer from the participant. Kate had been intuitively right to challenge him to join her.

Even after Joseph had recognized this, he resisted it, seeking safety behind the wall, which became for him a symbol of the barrier within, the peephole his only access to that other world.

Chapter 22

Lee went to Southampton.

On the weekend, Joseph followed.

From her one note, he knew she spent most of her time at the beach, so he had the taxi drop him at her club. Dressed in a new Palm Beach suit and a hat that made him look like a plantation owner, both bought especially for this trip, he strolled to the water's edge.

People lay strewn around. Underfoot were white pockmarked rocks which looked like tiny skulls. A dead sand shark about two feet long was washed up on shore. The gills and eye sockets were filled with sand. One of the club attendants shoveled it into a bag. He smoothed the sand with a small three-pronged rake that, handle and tines, was no larger than a man's forearm and fingers.

Lee was not on the crowded part of the beach. Joseph kept walking until he came to a relatively empty stretch. A fat man sat in a hole he'd dug, placidly gazing out to sea. Farther along was another man in another hole. And another man in another hole. Like most fads, it seemed bizarre to observers but not to those participating, who claimed that sitting in the damp holes was the best way to keep cool. Up and down this stretch of beach, a dozen men and women sat in holes of various depth, a few of them sunk in holes so deep only their heads and shoulders were visible.

The club's property line was marked by some pilings, what was left of a ruined dock. Their tops were covered with seaweed the green of the baize on a card table. Beyond the pilings was a crowd of younger club members, a few high-stepping in the surf, most lying on towels.

Lee, asleep, sprawled ungracefully. One arm curved over her head; the other twisted by her waist in what looked like an uncomfortable position. Her forehead, the bridge of her nose, her cheeks, and the tip of her chin were sunburned.

Sleeping next to her was a man with a thin mustache. If they'd been awake, holding hands, they wouldn't have seemed as intimate as they did asleep, side by side but not touching.

Joseph retraced his steps. He was so upset it wasn't until he got back to the city that he remembered he'd asked the taxi driver who dropped him at the beach to take his suitcase to Lee's house.

The following night at the whorehouse, Kate said, "You act like someone just died. Let me cheer you up?"

"I can't afford it," Joseph said.

"Bastard," she said.

She peered through the peephole and saw Joseph's eye.

"What're you looking at?" she asked, surprised. "Hey, give me a kiss." She put her lips to the peephole.

When Joseph didn't kiss her, she banged on the wall.

"I'm talking to you!" she shouted.

She put her lips back to the peephole. After a moment, she felt Joseph breathing into her mouth. The peephole was too small for their lips to touch.

She stuck her tongue through the hole. He touched his tongue to hers.

Abruptly, she pulled away.

Joseph put his eye to the peephole again.

Kate was on the bed, her hand moving inside her panties. When she tensed her abdominal muscles, her belly looked segmented like the bottom shell of a turtle.

"What do you want me to do?" she asked. "I'll do anything."

"Stand next to the wall," Joseph said. "On the chair."

She did, bending her legs so her cunt was next to the peephole.

"Don't you want to be in the room with me?" she asked.

"No," he said. "I want this."

"Ever since the first day, I'll bet," she said.

When he entered her, she started talking.

"This guy who comes here a lot, Shorty Rush—he plays with the Harmonicombo at the Criterion. You've seen him. He likes to tie me up. He took me to see his show this afternoon. This thing about Stephen Foster. 'Oh, de Camptown ladies sing dis song. Do dah. Do dah.' Awful. He wasn't so bad, though. He's got class. He gave me a bouquet and sat with me backstage afterwards, real cuddly. The other acts weren't bad. A magician kept pulling pigeons out of the air, but he smelled like pigeon shit. And this guy balanced on a wooden ball and juggled Indian clubs. All dressed up in a tux. He looked snazzy. I asked Shorty to introduce me, but he said no, the guy's a pansy. I don't believe it. I think Shorty was jealous. Then the screen came down. And you know how at the beginning of the movie the numbers go ten, nine, eight . . . ? Well, everyone in the audience is counting along. And Shorty said, 'They're jerks.' He doesn't like movies. Maybe it's because he always sees them from in back of the screen. Like we did. It looks the same, but it feels different. Like we walked right through the picture onto the other side of whatever it is: the jungle, the western . . .

"There you go," she said. "You're a real strange one," she added gently, "that's for sure."

As Joseph left Kate called after him, "Don't forget to put it in your notes."

She was mocking; but once Joseph got home, he did write up an account of the evening, although when it came to the part he'd assumed would be relatively easy in his case, the part that was possible only through guesswork and deduction in other cases, he was stumped.

He had no idea how he was reacting to living out a fantasy—which shocked him as much as if he'd discovered he cast no shadow.

He tried to read himself to sleep, but was too jumpy. He left the apartment to take a walk.

It was a sweltering night. Underneath his suit jacket, his damp shirt stuck to his back. The sidewalks were crowded. Most of the women wore light dresses or flimsy skirts and sheer blouses, which, sweaty as his own shirt, clung to them provocatively. Their expressions seemed either focused with arousal or slack with postcoital languor. All seemed available. Joseph wanted to make love to them all. And in his imagination he did, using the visible clues—creases and puckers in cloth, shadows—to create for himself the hidden naked bodies.

He felt privacy had been annihilated. In his imagination, he was intimate with the men, too. He could imagine them naked, doing things to themselves, to the women they were with, to other women, strangers whose paths they happened to cross. He was intimate not just with men and women on the street, but with men and women everywhere. His own sexuality ran from him like a current, connecting everyone with everyone else, and with animals, with plants even, peach flesh revealing its kinship with vulvas, the veined pouches of lady slippers with scrotums, the star bursts on the bottoms of apples with anuses; but not just these obvious correspondences—everything, everything that existed or had existed or would exist in the future, seemed caught in this sexual web, vibrating as though the very molecules, the very atoms were aroused. Joseph felt himself streaming into the night.

Back at home, he took three phenobarbitals. Then, growing groggy, he wrote to Jacob. After a few pages skirting the subject, he plunged in:

> From the beginning, I've tried to stay detached, to keep a scientific distance, to make no moral judgments. But so much of this sex seems violent and cruel—maybe it's true of all sex—that I keep wanting to judge. I have to judge. But as soon as I start judging, I lose all my scientific detachment, which is the only thing protecting me from getting involved.

Lee woke him the next morning. She was downstairs in the lobby of his apartment building.

"I'll be right down," Joseph said over the house telephone.

"No," she said. "I'll be right up."

She wore a metallic-looking tunic over a reddish skirt and a tight-fitting iron-colored cap.

"You look like a Roman legionnaire," he said.

"You look like someone out of a Degas," she said.

He wore white slacks and a striped jersey.

She stood in the middle of the room. He prowled around the circumference.

"Please," he said, making an openhanded gesture at the couch.

Lee sat primly, as Joseph used to when first interviewing the whores. She twirled a bead on her necklace one way and then the other.

"When are you going to pick up your suitcase?" she asked.

"Who was he?" Joseph asked.

"Who was who?" she asked.

"The guy on the beach," Joseph said. "Hell. It's none of my business. I don't even know you. Why shouldn't you go to the beach with some guy?"

"What do you want to know about him?" she asked.

"Everything," he said. "Nothing. How well do you know him?"

"Well," she said.

He slumped onto the couch, next to her. Across the room, in a small decorative mirror, they sat miniaturized. Both watched as though they were spying on another couple.

"What do you want me to do?" she asked. "Erase my past?"

When he didn't answer, she repeated, "What do you want me to do?"

Kate's words. As though she'd meant what Kate had meant, he realized he wanted her to do what Kate had done. In his imagination, miniaturized as in the mirror, he saw her lying on the couch, skirt up, legs spread.

"Get out," he said. He headed for the bedroom.

"You can't throw me out like that," she said.

"Please!" he shouted from the bedroom. "Get out!"

She followed him.

"What happened just now?" she asked.

"See those books over there," he said, pointing at the pile on the bureau—the large ones he took to the whorehouses, the medium-size ones into which he copied the amplified reports, and the various small ones he carried in his coat pockets. "Read."

She took the top one and opened it on the bureau. As though standing at a lectern, facing an invisible audience beyond the bedroom wall, she read aloud from one report after another.

"It's not science anymore," he said when she stopped. "I've become obsessed. But not with the sex. That would be simple. If I wanted to walk up behind you, as I do, and lift your skirt, as I do . . . You can fight those impulses. It's something else. Something harder to fight. I want to know. I want to know what would happen if I did lift your skirt. What would you do? What would I do? What would it feel like? It's not the sex. It's wanting to know."

"Do you want to know what I'd like you to do?" she asked without turning around. "What I'd like to do?"

"You'd better go," he said.

She left the bedroom. He followed her through the apartment. After closing the front door behind her, he watched through the peephole as she walked down the hallway to the elevator. When he realized what he was doing—more than that: when he realized he was responding as he did every time he looked through the peephole at the whorehouse—he sobbed, "Oh, God." He hammered his fists against the door, as though he were locked in a cell.

Joseph packed and took a cab to Grand Central Station. He bought a ticket to Galilee. While waiting for his train, he sat on a bench, writing a letter to Lee. His train was announced. He crumpled the letter and ran to call her. When she answered the telephone, he said, "Marry me."

"Joseph?" Lee said. "Are you serious?"

"My train is leaving in a few minutes," he said. "Answer me."

"In six months, if you still want to, I will," she said.

"I'll want to," he said.

"I know," she said.

"Then why wait?"

"How soon before your train leaves?" she asked.

"We can make the next one," he said.

"You scare me, Joseph."

"Very much?"

"Not enough," she said. "I'll be there as soon as I pack."

Joseph made a second call—to Jacob. After telling him about Lee, he said, "Remember once you said you didn't think you could understand an experience from the outside? You said that was always your argument with Dad. I want you to teach me."

"Teach you what?" Jacob asked.

Joseph said, "How to get inside."

BREAKING THROUGH: 1967–68

Chapter 23

On a mid-December evening in 1967, Jacob and Hermann stood in a field half a mile from the Old Campus, watching what looked like a star detach itself from the background of the night sky and approach. The light grew and split into two lights, one white and one red.

"Ezekiel's wheel," Jacob said.

It was snowing. His glasses, which had been steamy in the car, had frosted. The two approaching lights, glaring through the lenses, seemed to be made of concentric rings.

Hermann didn't wear glasses, so he didn't see the optical illusion.

"I would have thought the Star of Bethlehem more appropriate to the season," he said.

As usual, as soon as he spoke to his brother Hermann regretted the tone, although after so many years of squabbling they tended to ignore each other's hostility.

This time, however, Jacob, half in annoyance and half

in play, scooped up a handful of snow, which he squeezed into a ball and tossed at Hermann.

The snowball smacked Hermann in the temple, a little harder than Jacob had intended. Hermann reared back. There was snow in his mustache, snow in one eyebrow, and at the corner of his eye a tiny cut.

"There must have been some ice . . ." Jacob began.

Gloveless, Hermann scooped up some snow. His hands aching from the cold, he slowly molded a ball, trying in his methodical way to round it perfectly before he threw it.

"Wait a minute," Jacob said.

But already he was grabbing snow with both hands, making two snowballs at once.

The two old men were pelting each other when the approaching helicopter started to descend, whipping the snow into a stinging blast and forcing them to turn away.

When the helicopter had landed and its rotors had slowed, Jacob and Hermann were at opposite ends of the craft, so that Jacob's face, bathed in the taillight's glow, was red and Hermann's face, bathed in the nose light's glow, was white.

Joseph, peering through the helicopter door first at the red-lit face of his uncle and then at the white-lit face of his father, amused himself with the notion that he was being confronted with a devil and an angel like the ones he used to see in cartoons when he was a boy.

"You shouldn't have come!" he shouted to them. "You'll catch your death!"

In the dying whine of the helicopter, neither of the brothers made out his words, although both realized he'd said something. In response, Jacob automatically smiled and Hermann just as automatically frowned.

Joseph was returning from Washington, D.C. His studies on sexuality had made him first notorious and then eminent. During the past two decades, the government had been funding more and more of his research. His current project was a telepathy experiment, backed for reasons Hermann could not fathom, by the Navy.

Joseph crossed his scarf over his chest, buttoned his overcoat, and fished in his pocket for gloves.

"Where's Lee?" he asked.

"She couldn't come," Hermann said.

"Too cold," Jacob said. "Hermann wouldn't let her."

Hermann glared at Jacob, who flinched, thinking Hermann still held a snowball.

At Joseph's welcome-home dinner, Billy, Joseph and Lee's fifteen-year-old son, got tipsy on wine, and parodying drunken collapse, slid down in his chair until his chin touched the table. He always seemed to be sliding, flopping, dropping, falling, as though he were a visitor from a smaller planet and suffered from Earth's stronger gravity. Even before he was born, Lee had felt he was being pulled unnaturally from her womb. Three miscarriages had made her suspicious and superstitious. Although her doctor had assured her she was fine, she'd been convinced that her cervix was too weak to support the growing fetus, so she had insisted on being sewn up—like a Christmas turkey, she said. She'd been right; her doctor had been wrong. Her cervix was weak. In the fifth month, the stitches broke. Labor started, but was stayed when she was restitched, and she had to spend her last four months in bed on her back. Every so often—like when she saw Billy slip down in his chair—she still felt that her son lived a precarious existence, as though at any moment whatever was now protecting his life might rip and plunge him into death. Fearful of being overprotective, she'd developed a careless, even cold attitude toward him, which Hermann had adopted.

Ignoring Billy's drunken antics, she followed Miriam into the kitchen.

Billy waited until she was gone and then asked, "Can I be excused?"

Hermann, who'd been asking Joseph about his trip, broke off in the middle of a sentence.

"Why aren't you dressed?" Hermann asked.

Billy was wearing a T-shirt emblazoned with the name of a San Francisco rock band. He glanced for support not at his father but at Jacob, with whom he shared an unspoken humorous forbearance of Hermann.

"You're excused," Jacob said.

"Dinner's not over," Hermann said.

"Go ahead," Joseph told Billy, "but next time wear a proper shirt."

As usual, Joseph felt caught between his uncle and his father, trying to earn Jacob's approval by being gentle and Hermann's approval by being stern.

Billy ran up the stairs to his bedroom.

Miriam, swinging in through the door from the kitchen, asked, "Are you two quarreling again?"

Of the three of them, she bore her age most easily. Her lips had gotten plumper, more sensual than in her youth, and her hair, perfectly white, seemed blond, as though for her aging was not a process of stripping and exposure—as it was for Jacob and Hermann—but of putting on wigs and disguises. She put the tray of coffee cups on the dining room table. Lee followed her through the door, carrying a silver coffeepot and a heart-shaped trivet.

"What's he doing up there anyway?" Hermann asked Lee.

Lately, whenever she was in the room, he directed his conversation to her. Miriam accused him of flirting. He was. He'd always found Lee attractive and had always been attentive, but the previous year at her and Joseph's anniversary party she'd gotten drunker than he'd ever seen her, and she'd sprawled on his lap. Looking into his eyes, she'd put her hands on his cheeks (as she'd done with Billy when he was a baby) and said, "Did I ever tell you how cute you are?" Then she'd French-kissed him.

In all his years of marriage, he and Miriam had never French-kissed. The novelty of it, the broken taboo, together with the innocent way she'd held her palms against his cheeks, had aroused him so much that even after she'd staggered off to flirt with a colleague of Joseph's, Hermann was embarrassed to stand, something that hadn't happened to him for years. Acknowledging it to be an old man's folly, he felt like a young man.

Ever since, the memory of that arousal fed his growing infatuation with Lee. For the first time in his life, he felt truly in love. Gazing at the shadows of her braless breasts beneath her blouse left him feeling hopelessly jealous of his son. When she crossed her legs, his heart contracted. The cruelest surprise about old age—and the most pleasant—was that his feelings could be as intense as when he was a teenager.

"He's always in such a rush to get back to his room," he said of Billy, "you'd think—"

"A secret project," Lee said, fixing Hermann's coffee.

"Everyone around here has a secret project," Hermann said.

"Mine's not so secret anymore," Joseph said.

He brought out a copy of a tabloid newspaper he'd bought in Washington. A headline printed in red promised: SECRETS OF THE GOTTENBERG CLINIC.

"It's a wonderful story," Joseph said.

He opened the newspaper to an inside page. With a snap, he folded it back.

"Full of gossip, innuendo, libel . . ." he said. "The Presidential aide with the nervous breakdown. The Swiss banker's LSD cure. And—listen to this—'Superspies trained at the clinic's ESP lab . . .' "

Hermann grunted.

" '. . . will soon render even nuclear weapons obsolete.' " Joseph grinned. " 'Psychic warriors—' "

"Let me see that," Hermann said.

Joseph handed him the newspaper. Hermann said, "Look what they did to you." He held up a cruel photograph of Joseph.

In person, Joseph was handsome—handsomer than he'd been as a young man. Age had transformed his large ears, Roman nose, and jutting chin from slight defects into signs of character. Even balding had improved his appearance: his high dome, rising above the fringe of hair like a monk's tonsure, made him look holy. But in photographs he tended to appear arrogant. In the photograph chosen by the tabloid, he was grinning, his head tipped back. He looked like a Roman emperor who'd just seen a lion eat a Christian.

"No one takes this kind of article seriously," Joseph said.

"We shouldn't have this kind of publicity," Hermann said. "We shouldn't even be doing a project that attracts this kind of publicity. ESP lab! It's a waste of taxpayers' money and your time. Some crackbrained politician's fantasy. Superspies. Rubbish!"

He threw the newspaper onto the table.

"We're trying to find out if it is," Joseph said.

"I can tell you right now and save you work," Hermann said. Angrily, he picked at a wart on his thumb, as though it were a stuck snap he was trying to open.

Everyone else became still.

"Our subjects don't think it's rubbish," Joseph said. "They report very strong sensations, vivid images."

"But no conclusive results," Hermann said. "As for their 'strong sensations,' as you call them, you're simply using subjects who have a romantic, neurotic, and unscientific need to believe in that trash. What you need are unbiased subjects."

"Why don't you volunteer?" Lee asked.

Hermann gaped at her.

"You'd be a perfect subject," she said. "If you got results, we'd have to believe."

"I'm too busy," Hermann said. He hated turning down any of Lee's requests.

"She's teasing you, Dad," Joseph said.

"Are you?" Hermann asked.

He looked so hurt at the possibility, Lee didn't want to admit she was; so with a liar's exaggeration she said, "I've never been more serious in my life."

Hermann made a chewing motion to adjust his dentures, an old man's nervous habit.

"I'll stop by tomorrow," he said.

The next day after lunch, Hermann went into the basement of the new Main House annex, where Joseph's laboratory was. He knocked on the door's frosted glass window. A shadow appeared behind the pane, getting more and more sharply defined as whoever it was approached. It looked, Hermann thought, like a ghost coalescing out of thin air.

If there were such things as ghosts, Hermann added to himself.

Joseph opened the door.

"Show me around," Hermann said.

The laboratory consisted of eight rooms connected by a narrow corridor. At the far end was the test chamber, which looked like a meat locker. It had soundproof walls and a vault door. In it was a reclining chair, which looked like it belonged in a dentist's office or a barbershop.

"Now," Joseph said, "after I get you set I'm going into another room with Mr. Bloch, one of my assistants . . ."

He gestured behind himself at a stocky young man with blond hair, whom Hermann had neither seen nor heard enter the room.

"Mr. Bloch is going to choose a slide at random from our pool of over a thousand slides," Joseph said. "Some are in color. Some are black-and-white. Each is a collage made up of people, mythological characters, food, buildings, nature, animals—you get the idea. I'm going to concentrate on the slide he chooses. I'm going to try to send it to you telepathically. Now, look up."

Hermann did. In the ceiling was a glass window.

"I didn't see that before," Hermann said.

"Everything here is magic," Joseph said.

A face appeared in the window: a young woman with long dark hair, which fanned out on the glass as she bent toward the window. She looked to Hermann like a corpse floating in an aquarium.

"My other assistant, Miss Connolly, will be monitoring you," Joseph said, "checking your brain waves, you know, typical stuff. She'll also be taping you. All you have to do is relax and describe any images which happen to cross your mind. Afterwards, we'll see if anything matches up with what I sent."

The window went black. In the white ceiling, it looked like a shaft leading into the dark of space.

"Her light will be out, so you won't be able to see her," Joseph said. "Now we've got to prep you."

Joseph parted Hermann's hair and, using a cotton ball, rubbed acetone into the base of Hermann's head until it stung. He pressed an electrode in place. Then he cleaned and wired Hermann's earlobes, temples, forehead, and another spot at the base of the head. He taped temperature sensors to the thumb, middle finger, and pinky of Hermann's right hand. He pasted ping-pong ball halves over his eyes, which gave Hermann a dizzying sense of spaciousness.

Blinded, Hermann let Joseph seat him in the reclining chair. He felt helpless, like a stroke patient.

"I'm going to put earphones on you," Joseph said. "They're wired to your electrodes. What you're going to hear is the sound of your brain."

Just before he put on the earphones, Joseph said, "Thanks for doing this, Dad. I love you."

Hermann was astounded.

He couldn't remember the last time his son had said such a thing. He reached out for Joseph, but no one was there. Joseph and his assistant were already gone, leaving Hermann locked in the vault alone.

The noise from the earphones sounded like the crackling over a bad telephone connection. Still giddy from his son's parting words, Hermann felt his consciousness drifting up into some interior sky like a child's lost balloon, getting smaller and smaller until it was just a speck against the blank reddish inside-outside light of the ping-pong balls.

While he was being wired up, he'd been afraid he might not see any images. But suddenly there were pictures, as though projected onto a screen wrapped around the inside of his forehead. A field. No, a yard. With a triangle in the middle. A jungle gym. And something red in the lower left corner. A big ball. Like a beach ball. But bigger. A huge ball of yarn, which a kitten was playing with.

Images appeared and faded spontaneously. He described out loud what he was thinking, for the tape. He felt calm, drowsy. He hadn't been so relaxed in years. Even the crackling from the earphones was soothing.

At the end of the session, Miss Connolly pulled off Hermann's electrodes and ping-pong balls and led him into another room, where she projected slides on the wall. One of them would be the slide Joseph had been concentrating on. Hermann was supposed to look at them, pointing out anything that seemed similar to the images he'd seen during the experiment.

The first slide was of a sunset. Hermann mentioned the red, but it didn't seem like what he'd seen. The second slide had nothing that struck Hermann as familiar. The third slide was a collage of a lawn with a swing set and, in the lower left corner, a huge tomato next to a lion.

Hermann was furious and sickened, as though somehow he was being fooled—the same sensations he used to have when, as a boy, he would wrestle with Jacob and Jacob would suddenly give up and let him win.

"No," he lied. "It's nothing like what I saw."

As he left the laboratory, he slammed the door hard enough to crack the frosted glass.

That afternoon for the first time in years, Hermann skipped the pre-dinner convocation in the solarium of the Main House, the oldest tradition at the clinic—a tradition that Hermann considered virtually a sacred rite. Booted and bundled up, he struck off across a snowy field to walk out his confusion.

His puffy down-filled parka was snapped at the wrists and zipped to his chin. His hood, tightly laced, hid most of his face. Only his eyes were visible, peering through a small oval. His mittens looked like mechanical hands. He could have been an astronaut in a space suit, tramping through the wastes of a frozen planet.

By the time he came out of the fields at Joseph and Lee's house, he was no longer troubled by his experience. He felt light-headed and energetic. He wanted to do something extraordinary.

The brick path leading to the house was icy. On the front porch, Hermann stamped the snow off his boots.

From a distance he looked as though he was doing one of the primitive dances Jacob used to do as a young man. He was just about to ring the bell when Lee called out behind him.

She was coming down the hill, her knees plowing through the snow. Because of the ice, Hermann descended the porch steps sideways, leading with the same foot at each step, like a child. As he met Lee halfway along the path, he lost his balance. Grabbing her for support, he made her slip. To catch her balance, she grabbed him. Together, they toppled into a snowbank.

"Are you okay?" she asked.

"Just catching my breath," he said.

But he didn't get up. Instead, he scraped his hands back and forth in the snow. He was flooded with happiness. He'd found his extraordinary act. When Lee asked him what he was doing, he said, "Making a snow angel."

That night Hermann was unable to sleep. He fumbled for his bedside clock and brought its glowing green face close to his own. A little before eleven. He'd been in bed only an hour, but it felt like half the night. Every time he started to drift off, he coughed himself awake. After one particularly violent spasm, Hermann, afraid of waking Miriam, stole from his bed, dressed, and started downstairs. Halfway down, he was so overcome by a coughing fit that he sat on a step and leaned over, his head between his knees. Feeling suffocated, he went out for air.

It was a beautiful night. The snow, which had started around dinnertime, had stopped. In the moonlight the ice-covered branches glowed like neon tubes. As Hermann walked along the Galilee Road, he hummed "A Mighty Fortress Is Our God." Beyond the clinic grounds, a few houses already had their Christmas decorations up. Strings of lights outlined the door and windows of one house. Outside another house, a small juniper was so overloaded with lights it looked like the burning bush. On the roof of a third house, an illuminated Santa in a space suit rode in a rocket.

Down the hill, Joseph and Lee's house was unadorned. They didn't put up their decorations until Christmas Eve.

In an upstairs window, Billy passed. His light went out.

Downstairs on the far side of the house, Joseph's study was lit.

Hermann inched down the slippery driveway, crossed the yard, and peered through a window. On the rug of his study, Joseph, naked, was performing artificial respiration on Lee's prone naked body. Hermann felt himself go a little crazy. Where had they been swimming? Then he realized they were making love.

Hermann tramped back across the yard to the driveway. He'd left tracks in the newly fallen snow. In the morning Joseph and Lee would see that someone had sneaked up to the window and watched them. Hermann retraced his path, trying to step in the prints he'd already made. Then he backed across the lawn, trying to smooth the snow with his gloved hands, erasing the prints. It made things worse. Now it looked as if a crowd had sneaked across the lawn.

Hermann felt a coughing fit about to start. He hurried away from the house. As he coughed, he slipped; and coughing and slipping, he headed back up the driveway and home.

In the Director's House, lights were on downstairs. Hermann let himself in through the front door, scuffed off his rubbers, and in damp shoes and socks entered the living room, where Miriam sat across the coffee table from Jacob.

"Where have you been?" Miriam asked Hermann. "I've been frantic."

"I went for a walk," Hermann said.

"In fifty years, I've never known you to do something like this," Miriam said.

"The curse of regular habits," Jacob said.

Turning to his brother, Hermann asked, "What are you doing here?"

"I called him," Miriam said.

"Get out," Hermann told him.

"Hermann, he was worried about you too," Miriam said. "I had to stop him from going out to look for you."

"Get out," Hermann repeated.

"Let me make you some tea," Miriam said.

"I don't want any tea," Hermann said. "This is my house. And I want him out."

"It's my house too," Miriam said, "and I want him to stay."

Hermann stamped from the room.

Miriam and Jacob listened to him climb the stairs to the second floor and then on up to his tower study.

After a long moment, Miriam said, "I wish I could cry."

"He'll survive," Jacob said. "Nothing fazes him. He's like a man I knew a long time ago. A banker named Breck. He went bankrupt in the Crash and tried to commit suicide by leaping from his second-floor balcony. His wife was on her way home at the time. She saw him climb to the top of the balcony railing, sway, and jump, his frock coat billowing around him. He landed on his feet in front of her. He didn't even sprain an ankle. After all, it was only the second floor. He tipped his hat, which in the jump had slipped sideways, and without a word entered the house with her. To the day he died, he never mentioned the incident."

The house shook with what felt like an explosion.

Jacob and Miriam ran up the stairs to the study, shouting, "Hermann?"

The stepladder Hermann used to reach the top shelves of his bookcase had shattered the glass top of the coffee table. Hermann lay half covered with books. He must have slipped, grabbed at the books to keep his balance, and, in falling, kicked the stepladder across the room.

While Jacob phoned the clinic infirmary, Miriam knelt beside Hermann and took his hand in hers.

On Founder's Day of 1968, Billy's secret project, which he'd been working on since Christmas, was finished.

"You'll never guess," he told Hermann.

After Hermann had recovered from pneumonia and let Joseph take over the clinic, he'd become more approachable. Billy no longer was wary of him. And Hermann was learning to be more tolerant of his grandson's ways.

He'd lost a great deal of weight, and his legs no longer supported him. His hands shook so much, he couldn't feed himself, so Lee was spooning jello into his mouth. Some dribbled down his chin.

"Time for you to get me a bib," he said.

When he talked, everyone—even Jacob—tended to fall silent; his withdrawal from power had given him another kind of authority.

"Well," he said, "let's see this surprise."

Followed by Jacob, Miriam, Joseph, and Lee, Billy pushed Hermann's wheelchair onto the porch of the Director's House and down the ramp which had been built on one side of the steps. On the path to the Main House, Hermann said with his old testiness, "Just make sure you don't let go."

"You'd go flying," Billy said.

"Exactly," Hermann said. "And I'm a little too old to learn."

In the library of the Main House, now the Memorabilia Room, was a large table. On it was a model of the clinic as it was in a 1916 photograph Billy had found. The Main House. The Staff House. The Director's House. Even Jacob's old sweat lodge and the apple tree with the tiny colored ribbons and pieces of glass. On one branch was a minuscule mask with an eagle's beak. Standing beneath the tree was a balsa figurine, painted to look as Jacob had fifty-two years earlier. In the door of the Main House was Miriam. Hermann was climbing the steps to the Director's House. Rosa, on the back porch, was wiping her hands on her apron. Sitting at a window in the tower room, gazing out over the clinic, was Abraham.

"Very nice," Hermann said.

"Wonderful," said Jacob, who came to Hermann's side to look.

Carefully, Joseph and Billy fitted a large plexiglass shell over the model, and with a glue that Billy explained had been used to build rockets for the United States space program, they permanently sealed it.

Heaving himself up, Hermann grabbed Jacob around the neck. At first Jacob thought he was being attacked. He struggled for a moment; and then, just as he used to when they wrestled as boys, he gave up, surrendering to his brother's embrace.